A Christmas Hope

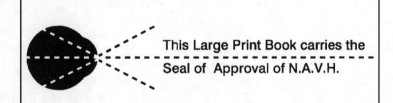

This Large Print Book carries the
Seal of Approval of N.A.V.H.

A CHRISTMAS HOPE

ANNE PERRY

THORNDIKE PRESS
A part of Gale, Cengage Learning

GALE
CENGAGE Learning®

Detroit • New York • San Francisco • New Haven, Conn • Waterville, Maine • London

GALE
CENGAGE Learning

LIBRARY OF CONGRESS CATALOGING-IN-PUBLICATION DATA

Perry, Anne.
  A Christmas Hope / By Anne Perry. — Large Print edition.
     pages cm. — (Thorndike Press Large Print Basic)
  ISBN 978-1-4104-6327-2 (hardcover) — ISBN 1-4104-6327-3 (hardcover)
  1. Murder—Investigation—Fiction. 2. London (England)—History—1800-1950—Fiction. 3. Christmas stories. 4. Large type books. I. Title.
  PR6066.E693C4686 2013
  823'.914—dc23   2013040142

Published in 2013 by arrangement with The Ballantine Publishing Group, a division of Random House LLC

Printed in the United States of America
1 2 3 4 5 6 7 18 17 16 15 14

To all those who would
carry the light

Claudine Burroughs did not look forward to the party. This November of 1868 it had been bitterly cold, the kind of chill that creeps into one's bones and makes them ache. Now it was early December and warm again. People were predicting the mild spell would last. Here in London there might not even be any snow! Most unseasonal.

Claudine regarded her face in the glass, not because she admired it, but because she must do the best with it that she could. She had never been pretty, and now in middle age she had not even the bloom of earlier years. She had strength, something not always admired in a woman; and character, also not necessarily cared for; but excellent hair, thick, shining, and with a natural wave. When her maid dressed it in a glamorous style, as she had this evening, it always stayed exactly where she wished. It was the one aspect of her appearance in which her husband, Wallace, had ever expressed his pleasure.

Not that that mattered to her anymore. He disapproved of too much that was at the core of her, like answering honestly when she was asked her political opinions — which were definitely more radical than most people's. She laughed at the jokes it would have been more ladylike to pretend not to understand. And, despite Wallace's disapproval, she worked at Hester Monk's clinic for sick or injured prostitutes — voluntarily, of course; she had no need of money, and the clinic had none to offer. She had begun there looking for something better to fill her time with than endless committees. Now she loved it for the fellowship, the variety, and above all, the sense that she was doing something of genuine worth.

She looked away from the glass. There was nothing more to accomplish here. She stood up and, thanking her maid, went out onto the landing and down the stairs, walking carefully so as not to trip over the hem of her rich teal-green gown.

Wallace was standing in the hall with his coat on. He was a big man, more overweight than his expensive and skillfully cut suits allowed to show. The flicker of impatience on his heavy features told her that she had kept him waiting.

He made no remark, no compliment on her appearance, simply held her cape for her and then nodded to the footman as he followed her out of the front door. Their carriage had drawn up to the curb ready for them. The coachman must have known the address to which they were going because Wallace did not offer him any directions.

They did not speak on the journey. They had long ago run out of things to say to each other about life or feelings, and Claudine imagined he did not want to pretend any more than she did. There would be enough of that when they arrived. The other guests were all socially important, which was the reason for their going. Wallace was a successful investment adviser to several people of considerable importance, and she admitted that he deserved his success. Apart from being gifted, he worked very hard at cultivating all the right connections. He never failed in anything he regarded as his duty. It was the laughter, the gentleness, and the imagination he could not manage. Perhaps it was beyond his ability, as well as his nature. During rare moments, she hoped he was happier in their life than he had ever made her.

And yet, it would be graceless not to acknowledge that she had never gone without any of the physical comforts of life. She had never dreaded that a letter or a knock on the door would be a request to pay a debt she could not meet. He had never lied to her, so far as she was aware, never drank too much, never embarrassed her in public, and certainly had never been unfaithful. She sometimes thought she might have understood if he had been, possibly even forgiven him for it. It would have shown a quality of passion she had never felt him to possess. Instead of admiring his rigid tidiness, it infuriated her. He folded everything, even the discarded newspaper, matching the corners exactly. He put everything away where it belonged as soon as he finished using it.

But that was a self-defeating argument. If he had understood passion and loneliness, the same desperate hunger for warmth, then she might have loved him, despite everything else. She had tried to love him. But here they were.

At least she could behave with

gratitude. She would do her part this evening: She would be gracious to the Foxleys and the Crostwicks, the Halversgates and the Giffords, and everyone else it was necessary to please.

They alighted at the entrance to the Giffords' magnificent house. Forbes and Oona Gifford were wealthy enough to entertain in the most lavish style, and seating thirty to dinner was no effort to their staff. Claudine and Wallace were welcomed into the hall, relieved of their outer clothing, and shown into the first of the large reception rooms. They had timed it perfectly: not the last to arrive, which would be slightly ill-mannered or self-important, but very far from first, which made one appear overeager.

Oona was Forbes's second wife, his first having died some ten years earlier. No one knew where Oona had lived before their marriage, and she never mentioned it, which was an interesting omission. She was very striking to look at, some might say truly beautiful. She came toward Wallace and Claudine now, her dark hair swept up luxuriantly and her slender gown the height of fashion. Wide crinolines were suddenly out. No one with the slightest pretensions to style would be seen in one.

"Delightful of you to come," Oona said with a smile. "Thank you, so much. In spite of the clemency of the weather, Christmas will be upon us before we know it. Let us begin to celebrate as soon as we can, I say."

"Indeed," Wallace agreed, forcing a warmth Claudine knew he did not mean. "What better way to begin the season?" He spotted Nigel Halversgate and moved toward him, realizing Nigel was standing with his wife, Charlotte — known as Tolly — only when it was too late to change course.

Oona saw what had happened and shot a surprisingly candid look of amusement at Claudine.

"Beginning to gain the Christmas spirit, I see," Oona said ambiguously.

"Such a party is definitely the best place to do so," Claudine replied, equally ambiguously. She was thinking of the discipline it took to be agreeable to a number of people she did not know very well or especially care for, but she certainly would not say so aloud.

"Goodwill to all men," Oona murmured under her breath. She sighed. "And women." Lifting her chin a little, she turned as Euphemia Crostwick approached, a delicately blond woman whose pretty face was always at attention, looking this way and that to be sure she missed nothing.

"I'm sure you know Mrs. Burroughs," Oona said, motioning toward Claudine.

"Of course." Eppy Crostwick smiled brightly. She looked up and down at Claudine's dress; it was a very handsome one, but it certainly would have overwhelmed her own diminutive figure, and its dramatic coloring would have bleached her skin. "It seems like ages since we last met," she added, letting the underlying meaning hang in the air.

"Indeed." Claudine inclined her head, her good intentions already vanished. "So much has happened. But surely it is one of the pleasures of life to be busy, don't you think?"

Eppy's eyes widened. "I had no idea you were . . . busy. Your charities, no doubt . . . You must tell me all about it" — she waved her hand delicately — "sometime."

"Of course," Claudine agreed. "I should be happy to. However, this is an evening to celebrate our own good fortune, rather than commiserate about the tragedies of others."

Eppy gave a sigh of relief, which was only a trifle forced. "I'm sure you'd love to meet some of the other people here. You know Verena Foxley, of course. Such a good-looking boy, Creighton, don't you think?"

They all looked over at the Foxleys. Claudine did agree that Creighton Foxley was handsome enough, if not quite as superb as he himself imagined — but then, Eppy had not really meant it to be a question. It was an opening for Claudine, who had no children herself — another way in which she had disappointed Wallace — to argue that Eppy's son, Cecil, was just as distinguished, in his own way. Actually, Cecil was very ordinary looking, but one did not say such things, for Cecil and Creighton were good friends. Occasionally Ernest Halversgate tagged along with them, half disapproving most of the time but reluctant to say so in case he found himself excluded.

Claudine took a deep breath. "Very handsome, in a certain way," she agreed. "But there are others perhaps a little more . . . interesting to look at, don't you think?" She smiled as she said it, allowing her implication to be understood.

Eppy was satisfied. "I do so agree.

Have you heard that Lady Lyall is to be married . . . again? The woman is quite . . ." She searched for a word.

"Extraordinary," Claudine supplied. It was the perfect cover-all word for disapproval that could never be quoted against you. Its entire meaning depended upon the expression with which you said it, the degree of uplift in the voice.

And so the early part of the evening progressed: a series of encounters with people Claudine had met on scores of other such occasions, from a world she used to be part of. But since her work in the clinic and her introduction to a different reality, it felt more alien than ever. Did she look as strange and lost as she felt? The thought occurred to her that perhaps everyone felt the same, in their own way; as if each of them were trapped in his or her own little bubble, jostling and bumping with others but never breaking through.

No, that was complete nonsense. There was Tolly Halversgate, elegant in the extreme of fashion, wearing a shade of purple-pink no one else would get away with. She was imparting some confidence to an elderly woman Claudine knew had a title of some sort, but she could not remember what. Countess or marchioness of somewhere. Tolly was a great royalist, always looking upward.

Lambert Foxley was talking business with a couple of hearty men at least ten years older than he. Both of them nodded to emphasize a point.

A couple of girls laughed just a shade too loudly, attracting the disapproval of their mothers, and the interest of several young men.

It was all colored silk, chatter, the glitter of lights from chandeliers, and lots of laughter.

Instead of mingling her way through the crowd again, as Wallace would have expected of her, Claudine turned away and walked through a garden room. At the far side she opened the French doors onto the terrace and stepped out. It was extraordinarily pleasant: a wide paved area extending all the way to the wall bordering the street. There were flower beds — bare now, of course, but no doubt full of daffodils or hyacinths come spring. There were also ornamental stone tubs at different heights, giving a most agreeable variety, and several attractive holly bushes. The terrace was overlooked by the windows of at least two of the neighboring houses, but they were all dark, leaving Claudine with an agreeable sense of solitude.

It was at that exact moment she realized with a jolt that she was not actually alone. Half in the shadows between the soft glow from the Giffords' lighted windows, there was a man standing watching her. For an instant she was frightened.

Then, when she realized he could only have come from the party, since there was no other way to reach the terrace, she was merely annoyed.

"Good evening, sir," she said coldly. "I apologize if I am interrupting you. I did not see you in the shadows."

"I didn't greatly wish to be seen," he replied. His voice was very deep and a little slurred, and yet there was a music in it, a lilt even in those few words. "Then I should have to make polite, inane conversation," he added.

She herself was not in the mood to be polite, or inane. Her eyes were becoming accustomed to the half-light now, and she could see him more clearly. He was of average height, which meant only an inch or two taller than she. It was hard to tell his age. His heavy hair was dense black, with not a touch of gray, even at the temples, but his face was ravaged by some inner wasting. His dark eyes were ringed with what looked like bruises, and his cheeks were blotched and sunken. His features were strong, his mouth generous, but already either disease or drink had marred him.

"That is what parties are for," she said, still coolly. "Polite conversation. What were you expecting?"

"Just one person who can see the stars," he replied, apparently not stung by her tone. "And you never know where you'll find them."

She recognized the music in his voice now. He was a Welshman, probably long left the valleys but never quite forgotten them. Surprising herself, she answered him honestly.

"No, you don't, but they are more likely to be found among those who are searching than those who would get a crick in their necks if they looked upward." She wished at once she had not said it. It sounded more judgmental than she had intended.

He laughed. It was a sound of pure pleasure.

"Well spoken, Mrs. . . . never mind, it doesn't matter. You will tell me your name and I'll think it

doesn't suit. I shall call you Olwen . . ."

She was about to object, then she
realized that she liked the name
better than her own. She wanted to
ask him why he had chosen it, and
perhaps what it meant, but that
would have betrayed far too much
interest.

"Indeed," she said quietly. "And
what shall I call you?"

"Dai Tregarron," he replied. "I
would say 'at your service,' but I
do little of use. Poet, philosopher,
and deep drinker of life . . . and of
a good deal of fine whiskey, when I
can find it. And I should add, a
lover of beauty, whether it be in a
note of music, a sunset spilling its
blood across the sky, or a beautiful

woman. I am regarded as something of a blasphemer by society, and they enjoy the *frisson* of horror they indulge in when mentioning my name. Of course, I disagree, violently. To me, the one true blasphemy is ingratitude, calling God's great, rich world a thing of no value. It is of infinite value, so precious it breaks your heart, so fleeting that eternity is merely a beginning." His bold stare demanded she answer.

"Wild words, Mr. Tregarron," she said, but there was no disapproval in her voice. She recognized his name. He was a poet of some acclaim; she was familiar with several of his works. They all had the same lovely, untamed feeling as the words he had just spoken.

"I'm a wild man," he said with a grin, and she found herself wanting to smile back. "Did you let them tame you, Olwen, put the fires out so you are never burned by them? Do you sit in the dark and the cold and wonder why you were born?"

"You're drunk," she said, trying to ignore the truth in his observation.

"Surely, I am," he replied. "Most of the time. Sober, I'm terrified. The world is too big, and I'm too small and too alone. Drunk, I can see only what I choose to. Can't walk a straight line — but what's so good about straight lines? Nature abhors a straight line. Haven't you noticed that?"

"The horizon is a straight line, at sea," she answered, wondering why she was even bothering with this ridiculous conversation.

"Ah!" He held up his hand to stop her. "Olwen — Olwen — the world is round. Did they not tell you that? And there are flowers in the grass where you have passed; you're just so busy looking ahead at your straight horizon that you didn't see them."

Suddenly she felt she must escape. She wanted to think of some appropriate riposte, but nothing came to her mind. She mumbled something about needing to find someone and turned away.

Inside, it was all exactly as she had left it: the laughter, the half-heard music, the glittering lights and the swirls of colors, all the faces she knew, and the others that were so alike she might as well have known them.

Almost at once Wallace found her. His expression was sharp with irritation.

"Where have you been?" he demanded. "I have some most important people for you to meet. I wish you would pay attention. We are not here simply for fun, Claudine."

"Just as well," she said quietly.

"I beg your pardon?" It was a demand that she repeat herself, if she dared.

"I said, that is just as well," she answered defiantly. "One should not go to a party simply for fun, especially at Christmas."

"Sarcasm is very unbecoming to a woman," he told her, taking her arm with an unnecessarily firm grip and leading her forward to meet the people he considered so important.

A long and joyless hour later, Claudine glanced toward the door to the terrace just in time to see Creighton Foxley stagger in. His handsome face was white and his clothes were torn, dusty, and stained with blood.

Claudine froze, wondering for an instant if she had taken more wine than she thought and that, combined with the tedium, it had affected her wits. Then she realized the buzz of talk was fading in the

33

room. One by one, everybody was turning to stare at Creighton.

One of the young women screamed.

Lambert Foxley made his way through the crowd toward his son. He was a lean and elegant man, a trifle austere looking with his perfect silver-winged hair.

"Good God, Creighton, what the devil's the matter with you?" he said angrily. "You look as if you've been brawling. Are you drunk, sir?" Then, before Creighton answered, Lambert took in the shock on the young man's face, and the fact that he was gasping for breath, keeping control of himself only with difficulty.

"What's happened?" he said more

gently. "Are you hurt?"

"No!" Creighton shook his head violently. "No . . . not . . . not much. But I think she's dead . . ."

Lambert Foxley looked as if he had been struck. "What? What are you talking about? You *are* drunk!" But it was a faint protest, made without conviction. He was beginning to understand that something terrible must have happened.

Now Verena Foxley was fighting her way through the bystanders, her head high, her elegant face twisted with fear. She looked first at her son then her husband.

"Creighton! Oh, my heaven! Are you injured? Lambert, call a doctor!" She turned angrily toward Foxley.

"He's all right," he said sharply. "Someone else is hurt . . . a woman . . ."

Martin Crostwick emerged from the crowd. He was small, neat, and seemingly in control of things.

"Come now, Creighton, tell us who is hurt and where. Take a deep breath and tell us what happened."

The words were given in a tone of command, and in spite of his father's clear resentment, Creighton turned to Crostwick.

"This woman . . . ," he began, his voice harsh with emotion. "I don't know who she is or how she got in here, but she and that . . . oaf Tregarron were quarreling over something. He struck her, and she fell back then came forward at him,

36

fists flying. He struck her again. We . . . we tried to stop him, but he was drunk out of his wits, and very strong. He was . . . completely beyond control. We tried to pull him off her, but I think . . . I think she's dead."

There was a moment of horrified silence.

Several of the women cried out with gasps or sobs.

Verena Foxley stood white and motionless as if she were turned to marble.

"Someone should call a doctor." Claudine broke the silence, moving forward to stand in front of Creighton, demanding his attention. "In the meantime, take me to this young woman. I have some experience dealing with injuries. I may be able to help."

Creighton stared at her.

While she waited for him to collect his wits, she thought rapidly about what might be of use. She grasped some clean linen napkins off the nearest table then a bucket of half-melted ice and a bottle of whiskey. If there were wounds to be cleaned, surgical spirit would be better, but whiskey would have to do.

"What are you . . . ?" Verena stammered.

Claudine ignored her. "Show me!" she said loudly and curtly to Creighton. "Now!"

Lambert Foxley called out something after her, his voice raised and angry, but she took no notice. If a woman was badly hurt, the sooner she was given whatever help was possible, the better.

Creighton led the way toward the terrace where Claudine had been an endless hour ago. He stumbled at the steps and put out his hand to steady himself against the door-jamb. He came face-to-face with Cecil Crostwick, who was pale and whose light brown hair was tousled. His shirt cuffs were also stained with bright scarlet blood.

Claudine was accustomed to both injury and disease at the clinic. Even so, she felt a stab of alarm. She pushed Creighton out of the way and brushed past Cecil and then Ernest Halversgate, who was standing almost in his shadow.

A young woman lay on her back on the terrace paving. Her fair hair was coming out of its pins; her dress was torn and the skirts all over the place. Worse than that, the bodice was crooked, half off one shoulder, and ruined by deep scarlet splashes of blood. Her face, bruised and swollen, under the caked blood, was ashen.

Dai Tregarron was kneeling beside her, a ripped-off length of her petticoat in his hands as he tied it around her arm tightly to stop the bleeding. Relief flushed his face as he saw Claudine. He straightened up and stepped back.

Ignoring him, she kneeled beside the girl and reached for her neck with the back of her hand to find a pulse. After a second or two she found it, but it was erratic, and she knew it could stop at any moment.

She took a cloth and dipped it in the ice bucket then began gently to wipe away some of the worst of the blood and dirt, looking for the other source of the bleeding apart from the wound already bound.

There were several cuts but none of them deep. Very gently, afraid of what she would find, she put her fingers to the back of the girl's head, searching for the wetness of blood, the sponginess of shattered bone.

The main wounds seemed to be the gash in her upper arm and another just below the elbow, as if she had tried to fend off a blow from something sharp enough to tear her flesh.

Claudine used the whiskey liberally and did the best she could with the napkins to make bandages at least adequate to stop the bleeding until the girl could be treated professionally.

She turned to see Lambert and Verena Foxley hovering nearby.

"Has anyone sent for a doctor?" she said somewhat peremptorily.

"Yes, of course," Lambert replied with something of his usual self-control. "And the police."

She had not thought of the police, but of course he was right. They must be notified. She looked around, and it was then that she realized Dai Tregarron had gone.

Cecil Crostwick and Ernest Halversgate shot quick glances at each
other. Creighton Foxley was standing close to his father.

"Who is she?" Claudine asked,
still on her knees beside the girl.

Cecil gave a helpless shrug. "Tregarron called her Winnie." He
looked at Ernest again. "We don't
really know her."

"I thought he said Winnie Briggs,
but I'm not certain," Creighton
added.

Lambert Foxley swore under his
breath. "What on earth is a woman
like this doing here, Creighton?"

"I don't know," Creighton said
defensively. "Tregarron brought
her. You'd better ask whoever in-

vited him. It all . . ." He gulped. "It all erupted out of nothing. One moment everything was good-natured, the next she and Tregarron were screaming at each other. We tried to stop it. He was really vicious, and we were afraid it was going to get ugly, but it was all so quick." He looked at the other two young men for support.

"He was totally drunk," Cecil said bitterly. "The man's a lunatic."

Claudine was overwhelmed with a wave of disappointment. Perhaps Wallace was right and she was a naïve fool.

She could do nothing more for the girl, at least for the moment. She climbed to her feet feeling heavy and awkward. No one moved to assist her.

"We should take her inside," she said to Foxley. "She'll freeze out here."

"Where on earth should we put her?" Verena asked, her eyes wide, as if the idea were made in bad taste.

"Somewhere warm," Claudine replied. "What about the house-keeper's sitting room? There'll be a fire there."

"I can't ask the Giffords' house-keeper to give up her sitting room to a . . . a woman off the street!" Verena exclaimed.

Claudine raised her eyebrows very high. "I was assuming that they would tell her, not ask her," she said very coolly. She expected a blistering reply but was angry enough not to care.

Verena's face flamed, but she turned in her tracks and stalked back into the great room. A few moments later, the butler came out with two footmen to carry the still-unconscious young woman.

Fortunately the doctor came within the next ten minutes, but it was a full half hour after that before the police arrived. They were led by a Sergeant Green, a soft-spoken man in his early forties who looked as if he had been on arduous duty all day and had expected to be home at his own hearth by this hour. Nevertheless, he was even tempered and conducted the questioning of the guests with courtesy.

The conclusion he came to was exactly what Claudine had feared it would be, but she could say nothing that would make it any different. Winnie Briggs had joined the party, either from a nearby establishment or off of the street, at the invitation of Dai Tregarron. Nobody else knew her, and unfortunately — but perhaps very wisely for his own survival — Tregarron had fled the scene. No one knew where he had gone.

Creighton Foxley, Cecil Crostwick, and Ernest Halversgate were all agreed that Winnie and Dai had quarreled violently. He had attacked her, and — in spite of the efforts of all three of the other young men to prevent him — he had seriously injured her.

She was removed to a hospital for the poor. Sergeant Green, having noted the Welshman's description, ordered that Tregarron be searched for throughout the neighborhood and arrested on sight.

In the dark, and in some distress and confusion, the party broke up and the guests departed.

"He should never have been invited," Wallace said angrily as their carriage jolted over the cobbles on the way home. "I can't imagine what Gifford was thinking of. The very best he could have got away with was a most unpleasant and unnecessary degree of vulgarity. Tregarron is a boor, and everyone knows it."

Claudine said nothing. She felt wretched about the whole affair. After her concern for the poor girl, the deepest hurt was her disillusionment in Dai Tregarron. Of course, he drank too much; he had not denied it himself, when they had spoken. But violence toward someone totally unable to defend herself was a completely different matter. Of what value was any poetic talent, no matter how beautiful, if you were capable of inflicting such pain on another human?

Perhaps she should have defended Forbes Gifford — or Oona, if it really was she who had invited Tregarron — but she knew it was pointless. In the early days of their marriage she had argued with Wallace, attempting to show him a kinder or more reasonable side to the things that angered him. Looking back, it was surprising how long it had taken her to realize such arguing was futile, at least with him.

"I expect it was Oona," Wallace went on. "Nobody really knows where she came from before marrying Forbes."

His condescension stung Claudine. She liked Oona Gifford, as much as she could like someone she hardly knew. In a sense, she was also an outsider. Without thinking, Claudine sprang to her defense.

"That is an unfair assumption," she said quickly. "She would hardly invite an unmarried man to an important Christmas party without consulting her husband, especially a man who was known to drink."

Wallace was startled. A magnificent carriage passed them, and in the sudden brilliance of its lamps she saw the surprise in his face. Then the darkness closed in on them again.

"Then you clearly know her better than I do," he said tartly.

"I know any woman better than you do," she retorted before thinking. She knew that it would have been far wiser to have given a softer, possibly also less accurate, answer. But it was too late to withdraw it.

"Well, even if Gifford allowed it,

you still seem to be saying that where judgment of men is concerned, Oona Gifford is a fool," he said coldly. "Hardly a necessary comment, Claudine. I had noticed. I think, if you recall, that was my original observation."

She was too hurt to retreat. "You remarked that Oona must've invited Tregarron, because we don't know anything about her past," she pointed out. "But you can't know that any more than I do. Therefore your conclusion that she is a poor judge of character is flawed."

"Rubbish! I thought Gifford had more sense, anyway." He dismissed the matter as finished.

"Or possibly Forbes has sufficient charity to extend his hospitality a

little more widely at Christmas."
She would not let it go so easily.

"Then he should have extended it
to us." He glared at her. "And not
ruined a perfectly good party by
embarrassing his guests with the
presence of a man like Tregarron,
not to mention one of Tregarron's . . . street women. I don't
know what morality is coming to
these days."

She thought to herself that there
was an enormous amount about
morality and human nature that he
did not know — an infinity of it —
but this time she did not say so.

They reached home in grim silence, dismissed the coachman and
footman, and went into the house.
After the cool night air, the warmth

of the house was physically pleasing, but she felt no sense of comfort at all.

Wallace picked up the subject again as they crossed the hall to go upstairs.

"Even at Christmas it seems we can no longer expect to see the values of a Christian society," he remarked, a step behind her.

She stopped abruptly, and he trod on the train of her gown. "I suppose you have been too busy with your wretched clinic even to have noticed," he added.

"You are standing on my skirt," she told him.

He stepped back, his face flushed with annoyance. It was clear in his eyes that he had no intention of apologizing. "I didn't expect you to stop at the bottom of the stairs. Am I to be obliged to walk around you if I wish to go to bed?"

"I thought you were about to explain Christian standards of hospitality to me, and I wished to pay it the attention it is due, rather than stand with my back to you," she answered, meeting his gaze.

"At this time of night?" he said incredulously. "Sometimes, Claudine, I wonder if you are quite sane. I don't know why the subject needs explaining at all."

"Because I was under the impression that Christian hospitality was meant to include all kinds of people, not just those we find most comfortable. I remember a number of occasions in the Bible where the Pharisees criticized Christ for dining with sinners."

His face flushed a dull red. "You are not Christ, Claudine, in spite of your charitable work for Mrs. Monk's regrettable clinic for . . . sinners, if you choose to use the word. You already spend more than enough of your time dealing with them. It is damaging your sense of values. At least other women might learn from such an experience, and place even more price on their own blessings. It does not seem to have had that fortunate effect on you. Perhaps you should direct your spare time toward other pursuits, for the foreseeable future."

That blow was deadly. It crushed

her completely into silence. She turned, and picking up the front of her skirts so she did not trip, she walked up the stairs, her heart pounding, each step feeling like a small mountain. She loved her work at the clinic. It had saved her from despair. She had begun it at a time in her life when the future spread before her like a long, gray plain stretching forever into the coming night.

She had offered her help, expecting to be given the genteel tasks of mending linen or making lists, and finding no reward in it but that of variety from her usual, desperately repetitive social routines. Instead she had found herself cooking in giant saucepans for dozens of hungry and sick women off the streets, even cleaning floors and heaving laundry around. She had used physical strength she was not aware she possessed, working past the point of what she had thought was exhaustion. She was caring for people in all circumstances, giving practical and emotional comfort without thought of herself — as she would have done for the children she had never had. Her mother had always called her selfish and incomplete. At last that was untrue, and the clinic had made it so. If Wallace took that from her, he would be robbing her of the most valuable part of her life. She should have kept her opinions of Christianity, and the Giffords, to herself.

Even now it would not be too late to apologize. Wallace was always pleased when she did that. But the words stuck in her throat, and she went up to bed in silence.

She did not sleep well, and when she woke in the morning she realized it was rather later than she had intended. She drank the morning tea her maid brought her, and dressed in a plain dark skirt and jacket. It looked a little drab, especially on a gray day, but it suited her mood. She thought about her few minutes on the terrace with Tregarron, the passion in his words, the blanket of stars above them, and the music of the party softened beyond the doors. It had been no more than a colored veil drawn deceptively over the hard outlines of reality. If such a man could beat a young woman to death, what were his wild words worth? No more than any other pretty lie. In fact, less, because they had passed so close to being a greater truth.

Perhaps it was a good thing she had overslept. At least Wallace was gone and she ran no risk of plunging again into last night's unpleasantness.

She ate breakfast, though she wasn't hungry; it was simply a wise thing to begin the day with a decent meal. She had just finished when the kitchen maid, Ada, came into the room. She was a pretty girl, in a dark, unusual kind of way, and Claudine rather liked her.

"Good morning, Ada," she said pleasantly. "You look worried. Is something wrong?"

Ada lifted her chin a little, as if preparing to face a danger. "Ma'am, there was a man come late last night, cold an' 'ungry. I gave 'im some bread an' a cup o' tea an' let 'im sleep in the stable, up in the 'ayloft where 'e wouldn't be seen. I give 'im bread an' tea this morning, but 'e looks that wretched, can I give 'im an egg or two before 'e moves on?"

Claudine felt a sudden warmth spring up inside her. Wallace would be furious if he knew, but this girl had exercised compassion anyway, trusting that Claudine would back her.

"Yes, of course you can," she said quickly. "And perhaps a little bacon as well. As long as he doesn't disturb the horses, he's no trouble to us."

" 'E in't no trouble to the 'orses, ma'am," Ada assured her gratefully. "In fact, 'e were good with 'em. Maybe 'e's a tinker, or such. 'E's real dark, like 'e could be one ov 'em, a foreigner, you know?"

"I'm glad you took care of him, Ada. Thank you," Claudine said sincerely. "It's a wretched time of year to be homeless."

"Yes, ma'am. Thank you. 'E looked scared, like somebody were after 'im." She turned to go.

"Ada!" Claudine said suddenly. "Is he hurt?"

"I dunno, ma'am. You think I should ask 'im?"

"No, thank you, I think I'll do that myself." She rose from the table and followed Ada into the kitchen. When the hard-boiled eggs and the bacon between two slices of toast were ready, Claudine took them out to the stable herself. If the man was hurt, or sick, it was very likely she had the ability to help. Since she had worked at the clinic she had learned a lot about people who were destitute, ate too little, and lived on the street.

She walked across the yard to the mews and then into the stable. She looked around for the groom or the coachman and did not see them. Thankful not to have to explain herself, in case either man should feel obliged to tell Wallace about the stranger, out of a sense of duty, she went into the hayloft.

"I have your breakfast," she said quietly. "If you would like it, please come and take it."

There was a moment's silence, then a man appeared and climbed slowly down the ladder. Claudine's eyes widened in shock. It was Dai Tregarron. He was still in his dark suit from the previous evening but now had dust and pieces of hay sticking to him and poking out of his wild, dark hair. He was conspicuously unshaven.

"Thank you," he said gravely, taking the sandwich and the eggs from her. He bit into them hungrily, perhaps for fear she would remove them again now that she knew her fugitive was he.

"How did you get away from the party?" she asked after a beat. She ought to have fled back to the house, she supposed, but she was rather curious. "The police were looking for you. That girl was very badly hurt, you know."

A moment's grief touched his face; he looked tired, and older than she had previously judged him to be. There was an air of desperation about him, and for an instant she felt a brush of physical fear for her safety. What was she doing standing here alone in the stable with a man who had beaten a street woman half to death, simply because he had lost his temper? Claudine was a tall woman, and fairly strong. But if three hardy young men hadn't been able to stop Tregarron, she doubted she would be able to defend herself against him. If he attacked her, he would be long gone before anyone came to help her. Ada wouldn't think to interrupt right away, and the groom did not know either of them were here.

"What are you doing here, and how did you get here?" she repeated more sharply, taking a step backward, away from him.

"In the dark I looked enough like a footman to ride as such on the back of your coach," he replied with his mouth full. "Don't blame your coachman. He's a gentle soul who didn't know the police were looking for me. Thought he was just giving some poor devil a lift."

She was confused. He had beaten Winnie and fled from the scene without even waiting to see if she was still alive, and yet he was asking her not to be harsh on the coachman. Her confusion made her angry, though. She resented the emotions he aroused in her.

"The girl is in hospital," she retorted. "She was still unconscious when we left."

His eyes widened: great dark pools of misery, depths beneath depths.

"I didn't do that to her, Olwen! Are you too innocent to see the darkness in three elegant young men with their scrubbed-clean privilege and their drunkenness of the soul?" He touched the darkening bruise on his face, which was half hidden by his black hair. For the first time she noticed the blood on him. "That's their work," he went on. "The blood is from trying to defend her from them, not hers to defend herself from me."

She wanted to believe him, but it seemed such an obvious thing to say. Why should he admit to beating her, even if it were true? And why would rich, comfortable, and responsible young men at a Christmas party with their parents have anything to do with a street woman?

Yet she wanted to believe Tregarron. It was perverse of her. Did she like him simply because he had flattered her, and because he, too, was an outsider, excluded in a way that matched her own sense of isolation?

"You'd better leave," she said, as if it were a decision she had suddenly reached. "I'll send the groom on an errand, so you can be sure he doesn't know you were here, or which way you went. The police will still be looking for you."

"What about your maid?" he asked. "Don't get the girl into trouble by lying for me."

"Do you think I'm going to tell her who you are?" she demanded. "To her, you're just a tramp, someone she was sorry for, because she's a kindhearted girl. Give me five minutes, then go."

"And yourself?" he asked, still without moving. "Or are you above the law, Olwen?"

She felt the warm color wash up her cheeks. "Are you going to stand there arguing and asking stupid questions or get whatever coat you have and get away while you can?" she snapped.

"I'll go . . . thank you." He said it with a bow so slight she was not sure whether she had seen it or imagined it.

Without speaking again she turned on her heel and went to look for the groom. She would find some errand that would keep him away from the mews for at least a quarter of an hour.

It was close to mid-morning when the police arrived. It was Sergeant Green again. Claudine recognized him from the previous evening, although he somehow looked different in the hard winter sunlight. He had with him a constable.

"Good morning, Sergeant," she said politely when the maid showed him into the sitting room. "Have you any news of the poor girl who was injured last night?"

"Not yet, ma'am," he replied. "She was in a bad way. I'm here because we're still looking for Mr. Tregarron. I don't suppose you would know where he might be?"

She did not have to feign surprise

at being asked so directly.

"No. I've no idea."

"You see, one of the other guests said you appeared to know him," he explained. "A Mrs. Crostwick. Said you were in quite close conversation with him."

Eppy Crostwick! Her jealous and troublemaking tongue.

"It was a party," Claudine explained. "As far as I knew, he was another guest. It is part of the function of such gatherings that one should make pleasant conversation with people, whoever they are. It is good manners and a courtesy toward one's host to assure that whoever else they invite should be made welcome. Certainly I had never met Mr. Tregarron before."

Sergeant Green regarded her a little skeptically. "Mrs. Crostwick said you seemed to know him quite well," he insisted.

Claudine kept her irritation in control. She was lying to the police about a man suspected of a very ugly crime. She could not afford to let emotion overtake her judgment. She forced herself to smile at the policeman in front of her.

"It was an agreeable conversation," she explained. "About beautiful and inspiring things. Such discussions cause me to smile. Perhaps she mistook that for a greater acquaintance than was the case."

"You met him on the terrace," he pointed out. "Alone."

"Good heavens! I know Eppy Crostwick is an inveterate gossip, but that implication is ridiculous. I went outside into the air for a few moments because the music and the crowded atmosphere were making my head ache. I have no idea why Mr. Tregarron was there, and I didn't ask him. We spoke for a few minutes, and then I came inside again." Deliberately she turned the barb against herself. "Look at me, Sergeant. Do I look like the kind of woman Dai Tregarron seeks out for an assignation on the terrace?"

Sergeant Green was clearly caught on the wrong foot. That was not the sort of response he had foreseen. He decided to retreat with what grace he could.

"I'm sorry, ma'am. Mrs. Crostwick is a bit unfortunate in her suggestions. I should have known better. I didn't mean to offend."

"On the contrary, you flatter me," she said with a faint smile. "I'm afraid I have no idea where Mr. Tregarron is. But please feel free to look anywhere you wish, to be certain. Just don't alarm my staff and make them imagine they are in any danger."

"No . . . of course not. Thank you, ma'am."

She went with both of them, showing them the entire house, from the servants' quarters in the attic to the wine and the coal cellars beneath ground level. She caught Ada's eye once, smiled at her, and moved on.

When he was satisfied, Claudine thanked Sergeant Green and his constable for their courtesy and for assuring that the household was indeed quite clear of intruders of any sort, either a fugitive from justice or a casual burglar. She bade them good-bye and watched them leave with a sigh of relief.

She sat down to a light luncheon with a feeling of peculiar exhaustion, as if she had spent the morning in some dangerous and highly energetic work. Dai Tregarron must have made good his escape, but she knew he was still in very considerable danger. Apart from Wallace — who she hoped would never know about the day's adventure — Tregarron also had against him the Foxleys, the Halversgates, the Crostwicks, and the Giffords. All of them would feel equally aggrieved by his intrusion into their world, even though someone had presumably invited him to the party in the first place. Whatever it was that had actually happened to Winnie Briggs, none of them would wish to be tarred by it, and they had the collective power to make sure that they were not.

What could Claudine do? Tregarron was free for the moment, but the police would catch him eventually. Maybe one of the young men from the party would tell the truth — or even poor Winnie, were she to regain consciousness and have any memory of the night! Of course Claudine assumed that the police would visit Winnie and ask her all the appropriate questions. However, if Winnie was the kind of woman everyone was assuming her to be, then the police were, on many levels, her natural enemy. Claudine, with her work in the clinic, would be a friend. If she wanted to know the truth, then the obvious thing was for her to speak with Winnie herself. Quite apart from that, ordinary humanity dictated that she go and see the girl, who, if conscious, was probably alone and feeling both frightened and in considerable pain. If she had friends they might well not know where she was. Or if they did, but were of her same circumstances, they might fear any kind of authority, enough to keep them from visiting her.

She put money in her purse, in case any purchases were needed — food or clothes, perhaps some small luxury that would ease her distress — then set out for the hospital.

As she arrived at the large gray building with its long corridors and its permanent smell of carbolic and sounds of echoing footsteps, she wondered who might have been here before her to question Winnie. Would Winnie even remember what had happened? Sometimes a hard blow to the head and a spell of unconsciousness destroyed the memory. Or, if Tregarron was telling the truth, what if Creighton Foxley or one of the other young men had already been here? Would they have persuaded her that it was not any of them who had hurt her? Might they have helped jog her memory with their own accounts and perhaps words of warning as to how difficult life could be for her if she chose to make an unwise testimony to the police?

Or, of course, there was the more humane but equally effective path of a monetary inducement to recall a few events just a trifle differently. Even something like ten guineas would be a windfall to a girl on the street fighting for every penny. Why would she forfeit such a chance?

And then there was the other possibility, the coldest and most realistic of all: that it really had been Dai Tregarron, blind drunk and fragile tempered, who had struck her, possibly not even knowing what he was doing at the time. To say that might not be a lie, just an accurate description of his drunken state, hovering between physical reality and the intoxicated worlds of the imagination, or the darkness where nightmares and vision collide.

Claudine reported to the nurse in charge, who viewed her coldly until she mentioned the clinic and Hester Monk's name. Then the response was quite different: a sudden flash of warmth. She was taken by a more junior nurse, who was hurried and overbusy, to where Winnie Briggs lay motionless on a narrow cot, one in a row of many others just like it. The ward was horribly impersonal, but it was both clean and reasonably airy, a legacy of Florence Nightingale's unceasing battle for improved hospital conditions.

Even so, Claudine was horrified when she saw the young woman lying under the stiff sheets. She was still unconscious, breathing shallowly. Her face was even more swollen now, and the bruises were black-and-blue. The blood had been washed away, but that made the extent of her injuries more obvious. One eye was closed, and

— until the flesh resumed its normal proportions — it would be impossible to see out of it. There were also bruises on her slender neck and across her shoulders. One could not judge her age, except that it must be between fifteen and thirty.

Claudine had seen many beaten women before. In the clinic it was a common occurrence: prostitutes punished by their pimps for laziness, theft, or simply lack of earnings; or beaten by dissatisfied customers who hated them, hated the world, or despised themselves for what they had become.

"Has she stirred at all?" she asked the nurse.

The nurse shook her head fractionally. "Not so far as I know, ma'am."

"Has anyone been to see her?" she pressed.

"Doctor's been to see her, but there in't nothing much he can do."

"I meant visitors. Police, friends, anyone at all?"

"I don't know. People come and go. I don't know as she's done anything wrong. Why would the police want to see her?"

Claudine knew the woman was tired, overworked, and probably underappreciated, but the question seemed stupid. She controlled her anger with an effort.

"Because someone beat her senseless," she replied. "That's a crime, no matter who she is."

The nurse shook her head. "That happens all the time," she said quietly, as if it were Claudine, not she, who was the ignorant one.

"I'm sorry," Claudine responded. "I know that. I work in a clinic myself. This was different. It happened at a party given by wealthy people, and a man is being hunted by the police for having done this. It's important that they get the right man."

The nurse looked surprised then sad. "Poor thing. Well, she hasn't said a word. Never opened her eyes, so far. I'm . . . not sure as she's going to."

Claudine looked back at the figure on the bed, and a coldness grew inside her.

"I brought a few things for her: soap and a small bottle of lavender water and a clean comb for her hair. If there is anything else she needs, or that would ease her pain, perhaps you would purchase it for her if I give you the money?" She pulled out the bag she had brought and passed it over.

" 'Course I will," the nurse said with surprise. "Who shall I say left it for her?"

"She doesn't know me. I was there last night and tried to help her a bit, that's all. I'll wait a little while, just in case she stirs. Can you bring me a chair to sit on?"

"Yeah . . . if you want." The nurse still seemed somewhat doubtful of her.

"I do. Thank you," Claudine said firmly.

Less than an hour later, while Claudine was still there sitting, half in a dream, Winnie suddenly began to breathe in a more labored way. She was almost gasping, as if she struggled to fill her lungs.

Claudine sat forward and touched the girl's white hand on the sheets. It was listless.

Within seconds the struggle became more desperate. Claudine got to her feet and ran to the main door of the ward, calling for a doctor, even though she already feared there was little he could do.

As soon as someone took notice of her and ran for help, Claudine returned to the bedside. Winnie was worse, her face as white as the sheets, her eyes still closed. Her breathing was shallower. Every now and then she gasped, stopped, then gasped again, as if the pain were overwhelming.

Claudine held her hand more tightly and touched her face as much as she dared, in between the dark, terrible bruises. She spoke to her, just saying her name over and over. She had no idea whether the girl could hear anything at all, or was even aware that anyone was with her, but she had to try to comfort her.

The doctor came, a thin man with gray hair and a weary face. There was nothing he could do, and within seconds they both knew it.

He looked at Claudine, looked at the quality of her clothes and the pain in her face. He did not ask her who she was. At this point it hardly mattered.

In less than ten minutes it was over, and Winnie Briggs slipped into the endless future of eternity.

"I'm sorry," the doctor said quietly as they stepped into the corridor. "I'm afraid there was never anything we could have done. She was too advanced in tuberculosis, and the beating on top of that was more than she could survive. But if it's any comfort, she would not have lasted a great deal longer anyway. A month or two, at best three."

"It wasn't the beating that killed

her?" Claudine asked. She was surprised to find her throat tight and aching. She was on the edge of weeping.

"Yes, it was," the doctor sighed. "But it only hastened the inevitable. Did you know her well?"

"No, actually. I suppose I didn't know her at all. I only ever saw her last night, after she was . . . beaten. I tried to help, for whatever that was worth."

"I'm sorry," he said again quietly. "You don't know if she has any family?"

"I've no idea. Probably not, or she wouldn't have been on the street. But the police will find out, I expect. If . . . if there's no one to claim her, I'd like to see that she's buried properly." She said it rashly, without stopping to think of how she would find the money, or what difference it would make to anyone. After all, the God she believed in cared for every soul, and what happened to the body left behind mattered not at all. But she said it as a gesture to the world that Winnie Briggs had mattered, just like anyone else, just like the people at the party so much more concerned about their own welfare than anyone else's.

The doctor nodded. "I believe you left a few things for her. I'll see they are returned to you, Mrs. . . . ?"

"Burroughs. But, please, give them to anyone else who might find them useful. Heaven knows, they're small enough."

"Mrs. Burroughs. Thank you. If you leave your full name and address, I'll see that you are informed . . . if no one else claims . . . Winnie Briggs." He sighed. "Now, I suppose I have to inform the police that she cannot testify as to who did this to her. What a mess. I'm so sorry."

It was a mild and very pleasant evening, but Claudine was unaware of it. Even had it been snowing and carolers had been at the door, she would have been unable to think of Christmas or any other kind of rejoicing. She decided to occupy her mind with writing letters but found her attention wandering, and what she was saying was far from the kind of happy message people wanted to hear at this time of the year.

At seven o'clock Wallace returned home. Over dinner he looked down the length of the carved oak table and regarded her with heavy satisfaction.

"The unfortunate woman died," he told her. "The beating he gave her must have been more violent than we assumed at the time. I imagine now you will not be so eager to defend him." He gave no preamble of explanation, as if she would understand exactly what he meant.

Indeed she did, but his words still

seemed to her unnecessarily cold.

"I know she is dead," Claudine replied without looking up at him. "I was there when she went."

"There? What do you mean?" he said abruptly. "Where?"

"At the hospital, of course." She was in no mood to cushion her reply. The situation still felt very raw: the pain, the sheer aloneness of the young woman, as if neither her life nor her leaving of it mattered to anyone.

"What on earth were you doing at the hospital?" he demanded.

Her anger was gone, washed away as quickly as it had come. "Visiting her, to see if there was anything I could do for her. I thought it very possible no one else would," she replied.

He opened his mouth to say something then changed his mind. He ate several more mouthfuls of roast beef before he spoke again.

"It changes the matter, of course," he said, staring down the length of the table at Claudine. "It's not just assault now, it's murder." He waited for her response.

"She was dying anyway," she said without looking up at him. "The doctor said she wouldn't have lived more than another month or two, regardless."

"You amaze me sometimes, Claudine," Wallace said with a wince of pain.

"Do I? Life on the street is hard. Many such women die young. So what is it exactly that amazes you?"

"It angers me" — he pronounced the words carefully — "that you, of all people, should say that since the poor woman was ill anyway, it doesn't matter so much that she was beaten to death a little sooner. I thought you to have some compassion, at least for the fallen ones of your own gender. I'm disappointed that you should be so . . . so filled with uncharitable judgment."

She put down her knife and fork. They rattled on the china from the shaking of her hands. "It matters that we use her," she said between her teeth. "It matters that we leave her on the streets cold and hungry. It matters that we abuse her, shut her out, that we mock her and strike her and then leave her to die alone in hospital. But it also matters if we charge someone with murdering her when they may well not have been solely responsible for her death. And it matters if we are sufficiently hypocritical to say it is murder if Dai Tregarron struck her, but if it had been Cecil Crostwick or Creighton Foxley who did, we would call it an unfortunate accident."

"You omitted mentioning Ernest Halversgate," he said with an edge of sarcasm. "Had you forgotten his name?"

"Ernest Halversgate hasn't the gumption to hit a rice pudding, let alone a living person," she snapped back at him.

"A rice pudding?" He looked at her as if she had taken leave of her senses. "What on earth are you talking about?"

"Hypocrisy. Did I not say so?"

"I think you had better go and lie down. The strain has been too much for you. You should attempt to do less. You are overtired."

She crossed her knife and fork on her plate to signify that she had finished. "I have done nothing at all, except sit with an unconscious woman while she died," she told him. "Perhaps if I had done a little more I would feel better."

Wallace smiled. "You are quite right. I'm glad you perceive that at last. You should busy yourself with the pleasantness of Christmas, keep up with the social acquaintances who matter to us. There will be more parties, the theater, and possibly the opera. It is a season of rejoicing. Perhaps you should see your dressmaker and get one or two more gowns. Something of a warm color would be appropriate. Not vulgar, of course, but perhaps less . . . less plain than you usually get.

"This whole matter is best forgotten as soon as possible. I'm sure the police will catch Tregarron sooner or later. The man's a drunkard. He won't be hard to find. You won't be called upon to say anything. The evidence speaks for itself. But if there's a trial, then no doubt Foxley, and perhaps Gifford, will say all that's necessary."

Claudine could think of nothing to say. He was talking about murder and retribution in the same breath as a new gown for the opera. It stung her like vinegar in an open wound, and yet she sat silent. She despised her own cowardice, but she also realized she had no words to rebut anything he said.

And who was to say Dai Tregarron was innocent, anyway? She wanted him to be, but she had no evidence of it. She was merely a naïve dreamer, without the courage of a visionary.

In the morning the newspapers reported that Dai Tregarron was still on the run, hiding from the police and now wanted for murder. They made much of it because his writing was admired by the literary establishment, even if his life was not. His best work, lyrical with his love of the hills and the skies of Wales, was quoted by way of illustrating how a brilliant mind had been destroyed by immorality and the abuse of drink.

They also pointed out that his flight had not in any way at all helped his case, and pleaded for him to come forward and surrender himself to justice rather than risk being injured — or worse — if captured by force.

Claudine never read the newspapers in front of Wallace. He had long ago given up attempting to make sure she chose only those parts that were suitable for women. Still, she preferred to read in private rather than under his disapproving eye. Today she was glad he had already departed for the work he did so well and so did not see how deeply the comments distressed her. He would have lectured her on the foolishness of concerning herself with people who were both socially and morally beneath her. He might have added, yet again, that she should occupy herself with suitable preparations for Christmas.

Even more dangerous was the risk that he would use the intensity of her reactions to this tragedy to end her work at the clinic. She could imagine the satisfaction in his face as he told her it was entirely for her own good.

She had tried before to tell him how important it was to her, and his incomprehension had wounded her far more than he had realized. It had left her with an awareness that underneath the outward trappings of marriage, the obligations of law and society, they shared almost nothing.

She despised herself for retreating from him, but it was a matter of preserving herself, keeping the small flame of hope alight inside her.

And she was afraid for Dai Tregarron. Public opinion had already judged him and found him guilty.

If there was any doubt left, then the Foxleys and the Crostwicks would soon put an end to it. With poor Winnie Briggs dead, Tregarron faced the rope.

For more than two hours Claudine worked on household accounts and petty domestic problems, but her attention was so divided as to make it necessary to do half the jobs again. When she had added a column of figures three times, and obtained three different answers, she finally gave up and admitted to herself that she could not disregard the fact that she did not believe Dai Tregarron was guilty. She must at least attempt to help him. In a sense the die was already cast; she had lied to the police on the morning after the attack, when the case was not murder, although it was certainly assault. She could say she had not believed Tregarron guilty, but that was not an excuse for giving him food and then denying to the police that she had seen him. She could not even claim that she had been afraid for herself. He had been gone by that time, and they would know that as well as she did. Heaven only knew what motive they might attribute to her! Considering his reputation with women, she preferred not to entertain that train of thought.

But what could she do for him — and, for that matter, herself? Where could she find active or useful help?

There were only three people she knew of who could provide any sort of assistance. Ideally, she would've liked to go to Hester and her husband, William Monk. However, Monk was head of the Thames River Police at Wapping. He would therefore be obliged to arrest Tregarron if he could find him, and possibly even to charge Claudine with aiding his escape! All of which would also place Hester in an impossible situation.

Claudine could not do that.

The only solution was the one she had considered first and decided she could not bring herself to adopt. She must ask Squeaky Robinson for his help. Squeaky was the highly disreputable bookkeeper at the clinic. His past was unspeakable, filled with details even he would no longer discuss. At the time of Monk's first encounter with him, he had been keeping a large and thriving brothel in the buildings that were now the Portpool Lane Clinic. How he had been duped out of their ownership was a long and complicated story.

Afterward he had become the bookkeeper to the new enterprise as a means of survival. Monk had given him no alternative, other than losing everything and finding himself on the street, without a roof over his head or a livelihood, painfully vulnerable to his many enemies.

Squeaky had had responsibility

forced upon him, but in spite of his many complaints about it, he had over time become rather fond of it.

He had originally regarded Claudine as an ugly and useless woman, only accepted as a volunteer in the clinic because Hester hadn't the steel in her backbone to say no to anyone. Squeaky had learned his mistake in that regard fairly quickly. Hester had nursed soldiers on the battlefields of the Crimea, and he soon found that she had enough steel in her soul to equip an army.

Claudine he had learned to respect rather more slowly, and with considerable reluctance.

In turn, she had accepted him as almost human only when a sudden burst of compassion had driven him to rescue her from a rather spectacular piece of foolishness, which he had never given away to the others at the clinic. She had no choice but to be grateful to him for that.

So it was early in the afternoon of the second day after the unfortunate party, Claudine went to the clinic. This was more or less in keeping with her schedule, and at half past three she found the opportunity to speak to Squeaky Robinson in his office.

He was older than she, though not by much, but life had used him hard. His long gray hair was a trifle stringy and sat on his collar. His face was cadaverous, snaggletoothed. His clothes were those of a dandy with dubious taste: a very well-worn frock coat, a white shirt cleaner than it used to be before the advent of his new respectability, and a cravat that was definitely more expensive and more elegantly tied than those of many gentlemen of means.

She closed the door behind her. "I'd like to speak to you, Mr. Robinson," she said formally. She was feeling awkward already, and she had not even begun.

"If you're wanting to ask about the money, it's all right," he said defensively. "We aren't overspent."

"Good. But I'm not here about the money," she answered. How like Squeaky to be off on the wrong foot from the beginning. "I need advice . . . perhaps help."

He looked at her suspiciously. "There's no money to spare. I can tell you that before you even ask," he warned.

Since he was apparently not going to invite her to sit down, she did so anyway, in the chair on the opposite side of the desk from his rather large high-backed seat.

"I don't want money," she replied. "I told you, I need advice."

He was still cautious, and rather unhappy. "What've you done?"

She would like to have snapped back at him that she had not done anything, but if she did that, she would only have to retract the words later. As it was, this gave her the opportunity to tell him the truth.

"I have accidentally become involved in a murder," she replied, ignoring his horrified expression. His quill pen slid out of his hand and spurted ink over his papers.

"It appeared to be merely misfortune at the time," she continued. Now that she had begun, she was determined not to be interrupted. "A fight that became more unpleasant than was intended. However, the poor young woman died, so now the police believe it was murder. Although I think that that is overstating it a bit."

Squeaky stared at her as if she had suddenly turned into a monster in front of him. "God help us, woman! What have you done?" he squawked.

She gulped. "I have helped someone . . . I helped Dai Tregarron escape from the police, although I didn't know he would be accused of murder at the time," she explained.

"What did you think it was, for God's sake, if the police were after him?" he accused her.

She took a deep breath. "I told you, I thought it was just a fight that got rather . . . out of hand. The girl — Winnie Briggs — she wasn't dead then," she added.

"If she wasn't dead, why were the police after you . . . or . . . whoever?"

"Because it was a nasty fight,

and . . . and the wrong person was blamed. I think —"

"You think?" His voice rose higher. "You think! If you had anything in your head to think with you'd have left the whole thing alone and got the hell out of . . . whatever it was! You didn't think!"

She felt angry and vulnerable. She was already perfectly aware that she had not exercised the best judgment. It only made it worse that Squeaky, the one person who might have helped her, had nothing to offer but blame. She responded with the greatest insult she could think of.

"You sound just like my husband."

Squeaky paled. "That's a terrible

thing to say, Mrs. B. I'm cut to the heart!"

She consolidated her advantage immediately. "Wallace will not even consider that the wrong man is being accused, because the other three who might have done it are all rich, respectable young men. The man accused, Tregarron, he drinks too much, is older, and has a somewhat dubious reputation," she added for good measure.

His eyes narrowed. "And why is it you think this drunkard is not guilty?" He knew her opinion of strong drink and those who overindulged in it.

She was trapped and recognized his awareness of it immediately. She raised her chin in defiance, but finding the words was less easy. "Because he's a womanizer," she replied. "He has charm — in fact, he's notorious for it. Why would he resort to violence? It's stupid, and it's unnecessary."

"Oh, well," Squeaky said sarcastically, "nobody ever does anything stupid or unnecessary under the influence of drink. Everybody knows that!"

"He's a drinker, so he must be guilty," she retorted. "I forgot."

"There's no need to be snippy," he replied. "What did you do, exactly?"

His tone brought sharp and very unpleasant childhood memories to Claudine's mind, of standing in her father's study while he required her to explain her misbehavior and then be appropriately penitent.

"He escaped from the immediate scene," she replied stiffly.

"How?" he asked at once. "I suppose you helped with that, too, did you?"

"No, I did not! He came as a footman on my carriage, and I had no idea until the following morning . . ."

Squeaky's eyebrows shot up.

"Do you think I look at footmen's faces?" she snapped. "It was dark. The coachman didn't notice, and I certainly didn't. I ride inside my carriage, not on the footboard!"

"Then how did you learn of it the following morning? He wasn't still on the footboard, I presume?"

Having to be this civil to Squeaky Robinson was a high price to pay for anything. She would rather have told him to mind his manners and be about the job he was paid for. But she simply could not afford to. "One of the maids found him in the stable and gave him something to eat," Claudine explained. "She told me. I went out to see what she was talking about, and I found him. I gave him breakfast and sent him on his way." She took a deep breath. "When the police came looking for him, sometime after that, I did not tell them I had seen him."

"Ah. Who looks after your horses?"

"I sent the groom off on an errand. If he knew anything about it, either he has already told the police, or he's not going to."

Squeaky pursed his lips. "And where is this drunkard now?"

"I have no idea —"

"Good," he cut across her. "Leave it that way. If you should be asked by the police and they know he was there, say you didn't recognize him. You can't be expected to know every tramp by sight. Who the devil do they think you are? You found him sleeping in your stable. You fed him out of charity. You have nothing else to add. That's my advice." He smiled with satisfaction and reached for his pen, looking with disgust at its rather bent nib and then at the ink marks on the page he would now have to write again.

"Thank you," she said stiffly. "Now I need your advice to know what I can do to help him, to make sure that the police don't arrest him and convict him, if he is innocent."

He raised his eyes slowly. "You have just crawled out of the fire, and now you want to jump back into it?"

"I don't want them to hang the wrong man!"

"They aren't going to hang anybody until they catch him, and they may not do that if he has any sense."

"He can't live in hiding forever! And he shouldn't have to, if he's innocent," she protested.

"It shouldn't rain on my birthday either, but it usually does. There's nothing you can do about it." He screwed up one of the ink-stained sheets of paper and threw it into the wastebasket.

"When's your birthday?" she asked.

"February," he replied. "What are you going to do about it? It always rains in February."

"Are you going to help me prove his innocence?"

"No. I'm going to do something useful, like pay the bills. Leave me alone to get on with it."

She was disappointed, unreasonably so, and she was also humiliated. She had come in here and interrupted the scruffiest and most disreputable man she knew, a man who had not long ago run a brothel for a living. She had asked for his help, and he had refused her. Worse than that, she could see that his refusal was perfectly reasonable.

She turned and walked away before he could look up again and make some further remark or — worse — see that she was hurt.

Christmas was approaching rapidly. There were now parties, theater performances, opera, and ballet for those who either had such tastes or found these events were appropriate places at which to be seen. Claudine was of the former opinion, Wallace the latter, although he did like certain orchestral concerts, particularly oratorio — the only one she did not care for.

A couple of days after Claudine's conversation with Squeaky, she and Wallace dressed to join some friends at the theater for a gala occasion. Claudine did not have a new gown yet, so she chose an older one. It had been considerably adapted, almost recut, and she felt it was particularly flattering. She had always been tall, and since working at the clinic she had had less time to eat. Actually, if she were honest with herself, she had less time in which to be bored, and consequently eat cake and pastries. As a result, she was considerably slimmer than she had been a short while ago, and it became her.

Wallace looked at her without interest as she came down the stairs to where he was waiting. Then he noticed the peacock-shaded silk over the darker blue underskirt, and his eyes widened. He drew in breath to say something then changed his mind.

"We'd better hurry," he told her instead. "We don't want to be late."

The theater was already crowded when they arrived, with people greeting friends. The sound of laughter, the swirl of bright gowns, and the glittering of lights gave a sense of festivity, as much so as wreaths of holly, the sound of church bells, and the songs of carolers. It still looked like there would be no snow. How perverse of her to be sorry for that! Claudine did not like the cold and was always afraid of slipping on the ice, but the snow was like a soft mantle, hiding the ugliness of so much, allowing one to be willfully blind to it for a season. For a little while the world could be as one wished it to be, reality painted over.

They were inside the crowded foyer, trying not to be jostled. She stayed close to Wallace. She would be most embarrassed to lose him, since he had the tickets. After a moment or two, in desperation, she took his arm.

She passed people she knew, at least by sight. She smiled at them and inclined her head. They smiled back. Wallace bowed. Once or twice

they made polite conversation regarding the weather or some un-
controversial subject everyone
could express opinions about without fear of contradiction. It seemed
unwittingly meaningless, and yet it
had some social value.

They took their seats, which were
in one of the better boxes, and
Claudine thanked Wallace for his
generosity.

The lights dimmed, and the buzz
of conversation ceased. The cur-
tains were drawn open to gasps of
pleasure as the scenery was revealed, and the drama began immediately.

Claudine found her interest in the
romance fading after only a few
minutes. It seemed clear from the

casting exactly who was going to fall in love with whom. And since the Christmas season was traditionally one of happy endings, the result also was predictable.

Instead she looked across at the people in the boxes opposite and, as discreetly as possible, began to watch them. She held her enameled opera glasses to her eyes, as if studying the stage, but actually looked to the side.

The first people she recognized were Martin and Eppy Crostwick. At this distance, Eppy looked as delicate as a bone-china figurine, with her flawless complexion and dainty features. Her pale yellow hair was piled up precariously. Claudine noticed a few other opera glasses trained in her direction, which would no doubt please her. Eppy loved to cut a dash, and her ambition knew no bounds.

Martin was sitting next to her proprietorially, looking self-satisfied and nodding his head now and then.

A little farther along, at the same level, were Lambert and Verena Foxley. They were speaking to each other and not even affecting to look at the stage.

Claudine was irritated with them for their ill manners. Then, aware of her own hypocrisy, she turned to watch the performance.

Half an hour later, when the plot was proceeding exactly as she had foreseen, she looked along the boxes again. This time she saw something she had not expected: Alphonsine Gifford was staring at the stage as if captivated by the actors. Her face was less beautiful than that of her stepmother, but there was a warmth and a charm in it that was easily as attractive. Her hair had a touch of auburn, which some people might not have cared for but which Claudine thought was particularly pleasing. Alphonsine had dressed in soft colors, which made her vitality even more apparent.

Next to her was Ernest Halversgate. He was a total contrast to her. There was nothing unpredictable in him. Some might have considered him good-looking, but Claudine found him insipid. Watching him now as he stared not at the stage but at Alphonsine, it was difficult to re-create in her mind the horrified expression that had been on his face as he stood on the terrace near Winnie's unconscious body. There seemed to be a faint smugness in him now. Could he possibly have dismissed it from his mind so soon?

Or was Claudine being totally unfair, judging him for what was nothing more than a masterful effort to behave with consideration toward the young woman he was accompanying now? From everything Claudine knew, it would be an eminently suitable match. Both sets of parents would approve it.

For the Halversgates, it would be something of a catch. Alphonsine was an heiress of substance. For the Giffords, well, Ernest had a reputation for diligence and sobriety. He might bore Alphonsine to death, but he would never break the rules, either morally or socially, and he would invest her money profitably. He neither gambled nor drank.

Claudine pulled herself up sharply. She was being horribly unfair, and unkind. She did not know Ernest Halversgate. Plenty of people who were interesting and witty were also cruel, and what good was all the entertainment in the world without kindness? She should stop making assumptions about his personality. Dutifully she looked back at the stage until the intermission.

She had not wished to meet the Foxleys and the Crostwicks, but Wallace did, so it was unavoidable. She should have expected it. It was very possibly why they were here in the first place. The romantic comedy was hardly to Wallace's taste, and she knew of no reason why he would imagine it was hers.

Close up, Eppy looked even more striking. Claudine was pleased she had worn something so unusual herself. Her height made her additionally noticeable, and in a manner quite uncharacteristic for her, she enjoyed being noticed.

"How extremely well you look." Eppy said it in a tone of voice that was hardly complimentary, as if Claudine had been fading away the last time they had met.

"How generous of you," Claudine murmured, meaning anything one cared to attribute to it.

Verena Foxley smiled as if nothing ever troubled her. She was rather like a swan gliding above the water, Claudine thought. Such elegant and regal birds, but heaven only knew what their feet were doing beneath the surface.

"What a delightful occasion," Claudine went on. It was only fair to Wallace that at least she try. "It quite puts me in the mood for Christmas."

"I was already in the mood for Christmas," Eppy said, with her eyebrows arched in surprise.

"So I observe," Verena murmured, glancing at Eppy's hair.

Claudine had a ridiculous image of the whole coiffure decked with tinsel and candles, and the desire to laugh was so overwhelming she snatched a handkerchief from her reticule and buried her face in it as if she had a fit of uncontrollable sneezing. She dared not look at Verena.

"I've heard no news of that wretched man Tregarron, have you, Burroughs?" Martin Crostwick said with a gesture of distaste. "I don't know why the devil the police can't catch him. It would seem simple enough. Dammit, even if he wasn't dangerous, the man's a bad influence on others. I can't understand it, but young men are apparently fools enough to admire his . . . I don't know what! Disregard for anything to do with decency."

"Don't worry," Eppy comforted him. "Their attention has been well and truly curtailed, and it was slight enough anyway. Tregarron's a fugitive now, and no one will give him food or shelter, let alone friendship. I think the whole miserable disaster happened at a very fortunate time. Decent young men will have had a sharp lesson against keeping bad company." She looked pointedly at Claudine.

Claudine wanted to come up with some scathing reply about fair trial and assumption of innocence, but no coherent words came to her quickly enough.

"I daresay, he'll leave the country," Wallace put in, perhaps afraid that Claudine was going to speak. He avoided looking at her. "After this, there's really nothing left for him in England. All he has is his reputation, and that's gone, as it deserves to be. A lot of it was built on hot air anyway."

This time Claudine did not stop to think.

"It's built on a large body of poetry," she said fiercely, "that is all rooted in the valleys of Wales, the hills and the coastline, the history. Even those with no Welsh ancestry at all find a familiarity in it. He'd die away from his own places. Where on earth could he go? He'd be a stranger always."

"Then he should have lived a decent life, instead of drinking himself half senseless and going from woman to woman," Wallace said extremely sharply. It was intended to silence her, and she knew it.

"Going from woman to woman may be immoral, but as long as the women concerned are willing, it's not a crime," she retorted. "And drinking too much is a vice practiced by half the men in London, at one time or another in their lives. I daresay, it is the same in Paris or Rome or anywhere else."

"Why on earth are you defending him?" Verena said in surprise. "You saw what he did to that poor young woman. She might be of . . . no virtue . . . but she didn't deserve that. I thought your charity work was precisely concerned with protecting women of her sort, at least from disease and attack."

"It is." Claudine felt the heat burn in her face. "And I'm not defending him. If he did that to her, intentionally, then he deserves to be put in prison. But we —"

Wallace lost his temper. He turned toward her with his eyes blazing. "There are no 'buts,' Claudine," he said between clenched jaws. "These highly respectable young men, known to all of us here for years, saw him do it and tried their best to prevent him. What happened is not open to question."

"Three of them?" she responded recklessly, knowing she would pay for it later. "All younger than Mr. Tregarron, and sober, and they couldn't stop him? He must have superhuman strength. I hope if they find him they get at least six policemen to capture him. Otherwise one of them may end up dead, too, like poor Winnie Briggs."

"Who is Winnie Briggs?" Martin Crostwick asked with a blank look on his face.

"The girl Tregarron murdered!" Eppy snapped at him.

"The girl Tregarron attacked in a drunken rage," Lambert Foxley corrected her. He shot an irritated glance at Claudine. "Perhaps we should not preempt a jury by leaping to conclusions. Although I don't see an alternative one, myself," he added. "The sooner the issue is decided, the better it will be for all of us. If I have a word with the appropriate authorities, perhaps we can avoid the necessity of having to appear in court ourselves. A sworn testimony should be sufficient, if it is clear enough that we all agree as to the facts."

"An excellent solution," Martin Crostwick agreed. "Get the matter over with."

The bell rang to warn that the intermission was nearly over, and without further comment — apart from general observations as to how pleasant it was to have met —

they returned to their boxes.

The rest of the evening passed by Claudine. Her mind raced, searching desperately for a way to stop Lambert Foxley from essentially ending the pursuit of truth before it even began, which is what would happen if he "had a word" with the authorities. Squeaky Robinson had refused to help. What could she do alone? She certainly could not find Dai Tregarron and warn him. She could not even look in the places Squeaky could have, or ask the people he knew. But she could ask the women who came and went at the clinic if they knew anything of Cecil Crostwick or Creighton Foxley. And Ernest Halversgate, she supposed, though he seemed more a spectator than a participant in the seamier sides of life. She would hate doing it. It was an unfair pressure to question the injured who came for help, but it was the last option she had left.

And she might learn something of Winnie Briggs that could prove useful, even if it were no more than the name of a prior acquaintance. Anything that kept open the questions surrounding her death would be worth it.

Blast Squeaky Robinson for his stubbornness!

Maybe she could give it one more try? If she went to see him with specific ideas, that might persuade him!

"No," Squeaky said even before she had finished speaking. He looked down at his ledgers, which were spread out on the desk in front of him. "We could use more money for supplies — medical supplies," he emphasized.

"We have plenty," she replied. "At least until mid-January."

"Not if we get a lot of patients in, and people have overspent themselves for Christmas," he said doggedly. "Then what'll you do, eh?"

"Go out and find some money, of course," she told him tartly. "As I always do."

"Very right an' proper," he nodded. "So go do it."

"By then Dai Tregarron could be in jail waiting to be hanged!"

Always literal when he wanted to be, Squeaky gave her a long, cold stare, and spoke very clearly. "It is December; Christmas is in less than a fortnight. They haven't even caught him yet. They've got to try him and give him three weeks' grace before they hang him. You're good at sums — that's more than a month, at the very least. He has time. We don't. We need more money."

"No we don't!"

"Everybody needs more money," he said reasonably.

"You really won't help me?" She felt despair well up like a dark cloud filling the sky. She had tried to do something like this once before, and Squeaky had had to rescue her. The memory was so humiliating she refused to let it enter her mind.

"No, I won't," he said flatly.

She felt ridiculously as if she were going to weep. She swallowed hard, a loneliness crowding in on her from every side: in society, at home, now even here. It had been absurd, even pathetic, that a woman of her age and station should find her only real friendship in a clinic for women off the street! And now even at the clinic she was alone.

"Then I shall have to do it by myself," she said with as much dignity as she could manage. She turned and walked out of the office, leaving him sitting at the desk, a pen in his hand and a look of baffled frustration on his face.

Claudine walked the length of Portpool Lane and turned onto Leather Lane, moving south briskly but without purpose. She was angry. She was afraid of doing this alone. Mostly she was afraid of failing.

She realized how perverse she was being. She knew almost nothing about Dai Tregarron, except that he had a poet's vision and the music of words in his brain. He might very well be guilty of having beaten Winnie Briggs and given her the blow that had been the immediate cause of her death, at least in law. He might not have meant to kill her, but it was a foreseeable result — and a wrong and brutal thing to do. Yet he hadn't seemed like a man who would do such a thing. How could one person hold such violent and terrible contradictions within their nature?

Why was she wasting her time at all? And it was a waste. Squeaky was only speaking the truth when he told her she would be far better employed raising money for the clinic. He had not observed that she was on this mission largely to defy Wallace and all the people she knew who were like him. Did she even know why? Yes, she did. Dai Tregarron had called her Olwen, had spoken to her as if she were a creature capable of escape from the commonplace, not the pedestrian, middle-aged woman everyone else saw, incapable of imagination, even less of passion. He had seen who she wanted to be and given the dream a moment's life.

Someone dug hard fingers into her arm. She gave a cry of fear because the grip was strong enough to pull her to a halt. She struggled, looking around the gray street for anyone who would help her, but she saw only vehicles passing by, people hurrying, collars turned up. She swiveled around to lash out with her free hand as hard as she could.

"What's the matter with you?" Squeaky demanded shrilly. He had to let go of her and step back smartly as she swung her arm, stumbling forward with the impetus when there was nothing close enough to strike. "Who the hell did you think I was?"

She was furious, and horribly embarrassed. A man in a morning coat and top hat was staring at them as he approached. He moved aside quickly, as if she might attack him, too.

"Why didn't you say something?" she shouted at Squeaky.

"I did!" he shouted back. "I called your name. You're so busy in your daydreams you didn't hear me. And you're walking like you're going to break into a run any minute. I ain't chasing you all the way along the street!"

"Keep your voice down!" she growled at him. "You're making a spectacle of us."

"*I* am?" he said incredulously. "I just touched you! You're the one galloping down the pavement like the devil's after you, then attacking me and screaming like a —"

"You were after me," she pointed out. "Well, what do you want? I presume you have something better to do than just scaring me half to death?"

"If me speaking to you in the street, in broad daylight, scares you half to death, how on earth are you going to detect where to find Tregarron and why he wasn't to blame for that poor girl dying?" he demanded. "You'll meet a lot worse than me in the first public house you go into."

She looked him up and down, from his cadaverous face and crooked top hat to his skinny legs in striped trousers and resoled boots.

"What do you want, Mr. Robinson?" she said coldly.

"To help you find Tregarron an' find out who killed that poor girl, you daft piece," he replied with total disrespect. "You don't have the first idea as to what you're doing."

She stood motionless, staring at him. She wanted to say something to freeze his impertinence, but she was also astounded with gratitude.

"Thank you," she accepted after a moment. She thought of adding something about his manners but decided against it.

"You're welcome," he said. "Not that it'll make any difference, of course. There ain't a damn thing we can do."

"Then why are you here?" she said tartly.

" 'Cos I remember the last time you set out detecting, an' how you near got yourself killed that time."

She did not say anything. There was no reply to make. Instead she asked him what he thought they should do.

"Look for that damn fool Tregarron," he replied, falling in step beside her. "Find out what he says happened, and then tell him to get out of London. Go hide in Glasgow, or somewhere else they'll never look for him. See what else I can find out about the girl, what's 'er name — Winnie Briggs. You should look into the doings of those three young men. And don't get caught at it, like last time!"

She did not reply to that, either, but kept walking, her mind already busy with plans.

Claudine began her own inquiries immediately, but it was much more difficult than she had imagined. She had to find a way to ask people about each of the three young men without appearing to be intrusive, or obviously implying that they were dissolute. That could not be done directly.

She wrote Christmas cards, a new

custom but a charming one. She shopped for small gifts to send to friends and the few relations she had. She bought a leather-bound copy of the history of the Napoleonic Wars for Wallace. All the time she was thinking whom she could ask the probing and extraordinary questions she needed to in order to learn about Cecil Crostwick, Creighton Foxley, and Ernest Halversgate. She had decided that the latter might not be as harmless and, frankly, as dull as he seemed.

In the end, she could think of no way to go about it but downright lies. She hated deceiving others, but she could do it without flinching; if there was a hesitation in her voice or a shadow across her face, it passed unnoticed.

She had already tried her best to question a few women at the clinic but had learned very little. It occurred to her then to speak to one of the patrons of the clinic, an immensely wealthy man who had been somewhat dissolute in his youth and who now made amends the best he could by donating very generously, to the clinic and other charities. She disliked approaching him on this subject, but she knew of no alternative. She would lie only to save him from the difficult moral dilemma he would have faced were she to tell him the truth.

"I'm sorry to ask you, Mr. Davidson," she said seriously. They were seated in his very pleasant study with the winter sun shining low through the windows and picking out the colors of the cushions on the leather sofa.

"Not at all, Mrs. Burroughs," he replied warmly. "Christmas is an excellent time to give to those in trouble."

"This isn't about money," she said hastily. "I have a friend whose son has lately become very close to a group of young gentlemen, and since then his habits and, to be honest, his character seem to have changed for the worse. I wondered if you could tell me, in confidence, if you have heard anything of these young men. Is their influence as she fears, or is she merely grasping for an excuse for her son's behavior?"

He frowned. "I'm afraid young men don't need much leading to go astray, if they are so inclined," he said ruefully. "I need only my own memory to remind me of that. Who are these young men?"

"Cecil Crostwick and Creighton Foxley," she replied. "Ernest Halversgate I am less certain of."

He pursed his lips. "Powerful families," he said quietly. "I have heard rumors that are less than flattering. Do you wish me to inquire?"

She drew in her breath to say that she did not wish it if it would be a cause of embarrassment to him, then she changed her mind and bit back the words.

"I would appreciate it profoundly," she answered. "I should

157

not ask if the matter were not serious."

"I'm sure," he said with a smile. He spoke gently, and there was humor in his eyes.

She felt a flush of shame rise up her cheeks. She liked Arthur Davidson. There was an integrity in him that made him the last person she would willingly have deceived. He was gentle, and he never made excuses.

"Thank you," she answered gravely. "It is . . . it is very important to me." Claudine rose to her feet, embarrassed now that she had committed herself so openly. "Would it be too indelicate to ask that I might know before it is . . ." She stopped, unable to finish the request acceptably.

"I understand." He rose to his feet also.

He did not understand at all, but she could not tell him so. She regretted that far more than she had expected to.

While she was waiting for his reply, she made very unaccustomed morning social calls on people who used to be friends in the most casual sense but who actually bored her intensely, and whose acquaintance she had let slip since working at the clinic. Fortunately, Christmas was the perfect time to renew friendships, possibly with a small gift of chocolate or candied fruit, and to swap gossip.

It was not difficult to ask about

parties, courtships, and who might be on the brink of marrying whom.

"A very nice young woman, Alphonsine Gifford is," one of her friends assured her. "My daughter is friendly with her. Less so, of course, since she has been courting young Halversgate." She smiled indulgently. "I know she has my daughter make a few excuses for her now and then, as girls will do, so that she can see him rather more often than she lets on. Of course, all the girls are willing to tell a little white lie for each other, now and then." She smiled fondly, and Claudine nodded, trying not to let her frustration show. All of this was familiar, understandable, and of no help at all.

■ ■ ■ ■

It was toward the late afternoon of the following day when Claudine was at the clinic checking on various supplies, that Squeaky Robinson found her in the small room where they kept the medicines. He came in and closed the door behind him. She turned around in surprise, at first not knowing who it was. She saw the weariness in his face, even beyond his usual rather haggard looks, and also what appeared to be very mixed emotions.

"I done a lot of asking," he said without preamble. "You want it straight? 'Cos that's about the only way I can tell it."

She put down the paper and pencil with which she had been making a list. She stood a little straighter, bracing herself. He was going to tell her Dai Tregarron was guilty.

"Yes, certainly," she agreed. "If you please."

"Tregarron drinks more than your average fish, enough so he should be as soused as a herring half his life," he said. "Takes his women where he finds them. Some o' the stories I heard I can't repeat to you. You pass out, I can't pick you up off the floor! He knew Winnie Briggs, all right. Liked 'er. Went both ways, from the sound of it. But she was a long way from being the only one."

He waited for her to argue, all but

daring her to.

"Is that all?" she said a little shakily. She had been half expecting this, trying to prepare herself. It should not come as a surprise. It was exactly what Wallace had said, not to mention the Foxleys and the Crostwicks.

"No, o' course it's not all," he said irritably. "I just wanted to make certain you got that. But I ain't telling you any more o' the details because it's the kind o' thing ladies like you shouldn't hear."

She was surprised, and in spite of herself a little touched, that he was protecting her. She had heard enough tales from street women here to think there was not much left that would shock her. But all the same, she did not want to hear them about Tregarron.

"Thank you," she said, being careful not to smile, in case it hurt his feelings.

He went on. "I can't find 'ide nor 'air of the stupid sod, which means the police probably can't either. So he's likely run for the hills. But I don't think he done what they're saying. He's a drunk, but I couldn't find nobody who'd say he was vicious, like. He'd fight a man, if he were pushed to it, and pretty likely knock 'im senseless — unless he fell over hisself first. Which has happened. But nobody ever saw him hit a woman. Use them, make love to them, then throw them away, surely! But when I say 'make love,' that's what I mean. Lot of talk, lot of courting them like he actually cared."

Squeaky shrugged, his expression mystified. "Maybe he did fall in love, or kid himself as he did. Every time! God help us. New one every few days."

Claudine was not quite sure what she felt — relief, confusion — and she was completely at a loss to know what to do next.

"But all three of the other young men said he did it," she pointed out.

"Whose side are you on?" Squeaky demanded indignantly.

This time she was obliged to smile, in spite of the bittersweet quality of it. "I'm sorry," she said.

"I think I'm on Mr. Tregarron's. And it sounds as if you are now, too."

His face was twisted with emotion from somewhere deep inside himself. "I don't go for hitting women, 'less they really asked for it. But if there's anything I hate like poison, it's some bleedin' wealthy little sod committing a crime and then blaming someone else for it, someone who can't defend himself, while he plays all righteous and walks away with his skin untouched."

"What do you think happened?" she asked, suddenly finding she respected him. In spite of his lurid past, he had a code of ethics, and he despised those who trespassed across it.

"I think those three little bleeders were playing with her, and when she couldn't take them all on, one o' them lost his temper an' hit her," Squeaky replied. " 'Cos she was ill, like, she took it harder than he meant. He got scared an' thought he'd really finished her. But she were still alive, and he panicked. Then he had to do her in for real. I think Tregarron tried to stop him, and all three o' them set on her an' beat the hell out of her and then blamed him for killing her. They're all out o' the same box, so they stuck by each other. Poor bastard doesn't have a chance against them, and they know that."

It was hideous, but it fell into

place, fitting exactly. Claudine could see it again in her mind's eye: Dai bent over Winnie, the bruises on her face and the blood, the stiffness with which he had at last risen. Maybe his injuries were not from Winnie fighting against him but from the other three as he tried to defend her?

"How can we prove it?" she said aloud.

"God knows," he replied in sudden defeat.

"They'll all have bruises," she went on, thinking about it. "We've got to get evidence of that before they're healed."

"No point," Squeaky told her. "They'll all agree that they fought. But they'll say *they* were the ones defending her."

"Three against one?" She struggled for a different truth. "They couldn't beat him?"

"He's used to brawls," he pointed out. "He's been in enough of them. It could take three fancy pansies like that to take him. I'd believe that."

"Then why was he bending over the girl to see if she was all right, not one of them?" she demanded.

He smiled very slowly. "That's a good one. But it won't make no difference, 'cos they're gentlemen with society on their side, an' there's three of 'em. But it does make you wonder, don't it?"

"Then we have to find more." She stated it as if it were self-evident.

"If they attacked Winnie, it won't be the first time they ever took a prostitute. There'll be history somewhere."

Squeaky's eyebrows shot up. "You think anybody's going to tell you that? What world are you dreaming of?"

"The one we both know, albeit from slightly different angles," she replied.

"I like your idea of 'slightly,' " he said with a wry twist of his mouth.

"All right, very different," she conceded. "I have made inquiries. I just don't have an answer yet."

"I'll look some more then, in the places I know," he said grimly. "See if there's a girl willing to talk."

"If you learn anything new, leave

me a message," she said. "I'll do the same if I find something."

He nodded.

Claudine began again the very next day. With Christmas fast approaching, time was too short to waste, even if it meant forcing the issue in a manner she would never have done in normal circumstances.

She contrived to get herself more or less invited to an afternoon party at a large house because she knew Eppy Crostwick was bound to be there also. She wore one of the new afternoon gowns that Wallace had suggested she purchase. She had seen it at the dressmaker's, and it had required only minimal alteration to fit her really very well. It had most attractive sleeves, lending her broader shoulders than she possessed by nature. Both that and the unusually warm color of it were quite flattering.

She arrived at the party to the poorly disguised surprise of several of the other people present, but she was made welcome enough not to feel uncomfortable. Not that discomfort would have prevented her remaining. She had nothing else to go on, especially considering Arthur Davidson might find nothing of value; worse than that, he might have agreed to assist her only to be civil, and actually have no intention of telling her anything.

Within moments she was drawn into the buzz of conversation. Gossip was cheerfully exchanged, and for the first time in a long time she listened with genuine attention. One never knew what one might hear; any small piece of information might inadvertently fit into the puzzle of Winnie's death.

It was almost an hour before she managed to speak to Eppy alone and not obviously be overheard.

"What an unusual pleasure to see you here," Eppy said with undisguised curiosity. "I can't imagine you are going to find many donations to your clinic, though. We are all too involved in preparations for Christmas. It always costs more than you think it will, don't you find?" It was a rather heavy-handed warning that she did not intend to contribute to the clinic and would not appreciate being placed in the position of having to refuse.

Claudine smiled back at her with a warmth she did not feel. "Actually, we are doing quite well, thank you. Many people have already thought of the less fortunate and given. A beautiful part of the true spirit of Christmas, don't you agree?"

Eppy's smile froze. "Of course. And how nice that you are not in the position of having people dread seeing you approach, in case you ask for something they cannot give."

"Exactly," Claudine agreed. "I would hate to embarrass someone who was in . . . straitened circumstances."

Eppy's smile turned to ice. A few yards from them, a woman in a silk gown whose cost would have fed a family for a year smiled happily and swept past to greet someone.

Claudine reminded herself why she was here and returned the warmth to her voice.

"But you are quite right," she said gently. "This is a time of year for enjoying all the blessings we have and being grateful for them. One can hardly do that with a long face or by thinking only of misfortunes. I do hope Oona Gifford does not feel crushed by that wretched event at her party. Until that moment, which no forethought could have prevented, it was completely delightful."

Eppy looked startled but hastily agreed. "I'm sure she will forget it in a while, especially if we do not keep reminding her." She met Claudine's eyes. "I imagine that wretched man will be caught sooner or later."

"He may have left the country." Claudine referred back to the remark at the theater. "That could be best for all of us, don't you think?"

Eppy thought in silence for a moment.

"I'm sure Cecil would rather not have to go to court to testify as to exactly what happened," Claudine went on. "Apart from anything else, when you have an interesting, busy life — as I'm sure he does — it gets harder to remember things as time goes by. There are so many other parties, other occasions."

"Yes," Eppy agreed. "Yes, of course. But I'm sure Cecil would remember. It's not every day you see some . . . some madman kill a woman in front of you." She shivered.

"Oh dear," Claudine said with commiseration. "Was that really what happened? Poor Cecil."

"Of course it was!" Eppy looked startled at Claudine's slowness of wits. "Tregarron brought the woman, and then when she refused to do what he wished, he struck her. Right across the face, Cecil said. He was horrified. He said that at first he was too appalled to do anything at all. Then when Tregarron struck her again, even harder, Cecil stepped forward and told him in no uncertain way that if he did it again, then he would be obliged to strike him back."

"Thank goodness he was there," Claudine said warmly. "What did the others do? Surely they were appalled as well?"

"Oh, yes, of course," Eppy agreed. "Cecil said Creighton Foxley was absolutely incensed. He tried to drag the wretched man off her, but apparently he had completely lost his head. Of course, he was out of his mind with drink. It took both of them — I mean all three of them — to drag Tregarron off. But by that time the poor girl was unconscious on the ground. Obviously that was all after you spoke with the man. Why did you go out to the terrace, anyway?" She looked at Claudine curiously.

"I went for a breath of air. It is actually a very pleasant space," Claudine explained. Nearly the truth. There was no need to say that the conversation had bored her and made her feel hemmed in by trivialities. That would be unnecessarily rude. Perhaps others felt as she did but had better manners than to let it be known.

"And you were the first one out after the . . . the tragedy," Eppy noted. "I expect Cecil was trying to revive her, when you found them."

"Actually . . . ," Claudine began then suddenly changed her mind. "They were all crowded near her when I got there. Poor Cecil, what a distress for him it must've been when she did not stir."

"Terrible," Eppy agreed. "I don't know how you think he could forget it in a few days, or even weeks."

"I'm sorry," Claudine lied. "I hadn't thought about it that way. Well, that testimony should be plain enough for there to be no defense for Tregarron."

"None at all," Eppy agreed.

"I imagine Creighton and Ernest Halversgate will say the same. They'd all be there to support one another . . . over the distress of it all, I mean."

"I imagine so," Eppy agreed. "And wouldn't you have to testify if that awful man is arrested? I mean, mightn't you have to?"

"Yes," Claudine said very soberly, "I would have to." She gulped air, and it caught in her throat, almost choking her. What Eppy had described was not at all what she had seen. But if all three of the boys swore to the same circumstance, would her word be enough against theirs? She doubted it. "Of course," she added when she had regained her composure.

The day after that she decided to pursue another tack. She did not know Alphonsine Gifford well.

However, on the occasions when they had met she had found her a very pleasant young woman and of an independent mind, which showed a degree of courage as well as intelligence. She decided to visit her and congratulate her on her prospective engagement to Ernest Halversgate.

They were sitting in the withdrawing room. It was the appropriate place to receive calls, traditionally known as "morning calls," although the visits actually took place in the afternoon. The fire was roaring up the chimney, in spite of the still unusually clement weather. The mantel was decked with garlands, as were many of the doors and archways. It all looked most welcoming. It took an effort of will to recall that only just over a week ago a tragedy had taken place in this house.

Alphonsine was dressed in an afternoon gown of rich burgundy, which was startlingly attractive against her warm coloring. Claudine would have expected the shade to be overpowering, but on the contrary, it seemed perfectly natural on Alphonsine.

"Thank you," the young woman said demurely when Claudine offered her congratulations. "I'm sure I shall be very happy." She looked down at her hands, avoiding Claudine's eyes.

With a jolt of memory Claudine thought of herself thirty years ago, sitting just like that, receiving some-one's well-meant congratulations on becoming engaged to Wallace. What her visitor had implied was that a girl as plain as Claudine was lucky to receive an offer of marriage from a man as decent and promising as Wallace. Someone safe, comfortable, and assured of respectability. And in truth, it was much more than some women could look forward to. Heaven knew, she had ministered to hundreds who would have given everything they possessed to change places with her. A roof over their heads, warmth, food, and nice clothes were dreams that barely flickered in their imaginations.

Poor Winnie Briggs had been one

of them.

That thought jerked Claudine back to her reason for being here, which had nothing to do with the fresh hot tea, cakes and tiny pies of pastry, and rich fruit that were before her on the table.

"I hope you will be," she said. "Of course, much of happiness is what we make of it. But I believe you are a woman of courage. You will embrace life. You will not expect it always to be gentle with you, or even fair."

Alphonsine's head came up sharply, and she met Claudine's eyes. "What . . . what do you mean? And don't tell me you don't mean anything. I know you better than that, Mrs. Burroughs. You are not one of the usual society women who goes from party to party, giving a little charity here and there and saying all sorts of things they don't mean. You work at the clinic in Portpool Lane, don't you?"

Claudine was surprised. "Yes. It means a great deal to me. Why do you ask?"

"Do you have women there like the one who died here the other evening?"

"Yes. Many exactly like her. We do manage to save most of them, and at least to give a little comfort to those we can't save. But if you're worried about Mr. Halversgate's part in all this, there's no need to be — I'm sure he did all he could to save her."

Alphonsine's eyes lowered again. "Of course. It was . . . dreadful." Suddenly she looked intently at Claudine. "Will he have to testify in court, if they find Mr. Tregarron? Do you think they will? If . . . if they find him guilty, they'll hang him, won't they?"

In spite of the fire and the hot tea, Claudine was chilled. She remembered Lambert Foxley's words about assuring that the young men would not have to appear in court and therefore would avoid being cross-questioned by a lawyer for the defense. Was it because he wanted to spare them the ordeal of a trial, or because he wanted to ensure they would not be caught in a lie? Apparently, Alphonsine did not question the story Ernest and his friends had offered. Claudine doubted the young woman would be able to sit calmly on a sofa if she thought her soon-to-be fiancé was guilty of such a crime and that it was possible an innocent man could be hanged for something he did not do.

"Yes," she said decisively. "They will hang him, if they believe he deliberately beat her. But Mr. Halversgate was there. He must know what happened, and he will be able to testify to it."

Alphonsine stared at her. "Yes . . ." She swallowed. "He will. But of course he was not the only one who was there. Cecil Crostwick and Creighton Foxley were as well.

Perhaps one of them testifying will be enough . . . do you think?"

"No, I'm afraid I don't think so at all." Claudine had no compunction in being blunt with her. "If you were the person defending Mr. Tregarron, wouldn't you wish to question them all, to make sure their accounts were exactly the same?"

"I suppose I would." Alphonsine gave a very slight smile. "Don't you think they will make sure that it is? If Mr. Tregarron is caught, of course?"

Claudine thought for a moment before she answered. "But, of course, they would have been standing in different places and therefore seen things slightly differently. So their accounts might be a bit varied."

Alphonsine was very pale, even in the gaslight. "I . . . yes, of course they would. I hadn't thought of that."

"It would probably be best if they each described exactly what they saw. One would wish to be as natural sounding as possible, should it come to anything, which of course it may not."

A succession of emotions crossed Alphonsine's face: relief, disappointment, then misery. "Yes, you are quite right," she agreed. "Perhaps he will never be caught, and they won't have to say anything at all."

In the hansom cab on her way home, Claudine considered all the bits of information she had gathered. Only one struck her as very slightly incongruous now, after talking to Alphonsine — the fact that the girl was having her friends tell what amounted to lies, even if very conventional ones, so that she might spend more time with Ernest Halversgate. The girl didn't seem particularly besotted, though happy enough. It appeared to be a relationship of convenience . . . So, surely the ordinary social arrangements were more than sufficient? It was a small thing, but it nagged at her. She decided then that she had no choice but to call again on Arthur Davidson.

She hated doing it. She was actually trembling as she stood at the front door and reached for the brass-headed bell pull, but she could not afford to wait any longer. If Arthur Davidson preferred not to answer her request, then better that she know it now. She was aware that by returning to press him for more information, she might also make him less likely to contribute to the clinic in the future. That would be a heavy blow. He had been generous.

The footman opened the door and recognized her immediately. A few minutes later she was in the withdrawing room in front of the fire, Davidson standing to receive her. She had always seen him in his study before, or at the clinic. How-

ever, there was no time to appreciate the glass-paned bookcase or the
slightly mismatched furniture, evidence that he cared for comfort
rather than for appearances. She
wondered what his wife was like.
He had never spoken of her.

Claudine forced herself to address
the subject immediately.

"I apologize, but I must ask you
if you have learned anything about
the three young men we recently
spoke about." She swallowed. Her
mouth was dry. "I am afraid the
matter grows urgent."

His mouth pulled a little tighter,
and there was a sadness in his eyes.
"I have. None of it particularly
surprising. Halversgate is, as you
implied, a follower rather than a

leader. Crostwick and Foxley are another matter. In better society, they are merely a trifle daring. More privately, they indulge in excess of drink in very dubious places, which increasingly often descends to violence. I wish I could tell you otherwise." A faint humor touched his mouth. "I would advise your friend, if she exists, to counsel her son most strongly not to associate with them. They may never be caught doing anything wrong, but they are a malign influence."

Claudine felt the color burn up her face. She was clearly far more transparent than she had intended.

"Thank you," she said awkwardly. She could not tell him the real reason for her inquiries, but she made no more pretense at excuses. She was too embarrassed to accept any hospitality, even though she would have enjoyed conversing with him on other matters. After wishing him a happy Christmas, she excused herself and left.

The next morning Claudine told Squeaky Robinson what she had learned. They were in his office with the door closed. The rest of the clinic was busy preparing for Christmas — trying to bring as much cheer as possible to those who had nowhere else to go, or whose sickness and injuries made them unable to care for themselves.

Squeaky was impressed with her account, although he did his best not to show it.

"Good," he said a trifle senten-
tiously. "It's a start. So Halversgate's a follower."

"Apparently. This is information,
but I'm afraid it is not proof," she
warned.

Squeaky pulled his face into an
expression of disgust. "I know that!
But don't underestimate it. It'll
give you a lever to use with him."

"Me?" She was startled. "How?"

He squinted at her. "He doesn't
know you don't have proof. We
can't neither of us find anything
much about Winnie Briggs, poor
little cow. Nothing different from
thousands of others, just unlucky.
An' so far I still haven't found any
sign of Tregarron, just a lot of
stories, most of 'em lies, far as I

can tell. But it only needs one nasty bastard rubbed the wrong way, an' someone'll nab him. So you'd better get about it, seeing as I can't hardly go, and put a flea in Mr. Halversgate's tail. You'll think of something."

Claudine did not find this task easy. She hated not so much actually telling a lie, but rather implying one and allowing it to be understood. Ordinary tact in talking about things that did not matter greatly was a social skill everyone was expected to possess. But deception came hard to her. Social exchange was a web of small flatteries and of compromises that entangled them all. It was one of the reasons she found it difficult.

Nevertheless, she needed to speak honestly with Ernest Halversgate.

While ostensibly calling on Tolly Halversgate, she actually met with Ernest in the large garden room overlooking their paved terrace and the rather fine balustrade, which gave the illusion that the lawn was bigger than it actually was. It was a clever piece of design, and she admired it.

"Thank you," Ernest said a little stiffly. "My grandfather had it put in. It was rather dull before. I'm so sorry Mama is not here, Mrs. Burroughs. I don't expect her for another half hour or so." He was a very correct young man and at the moment clearly embarrassed.

Claudine smiled at him. "I'm sure

it is my fault. I must have written down the wrong time. Or else I have it confused with another date. If I improved my handwriting, instead of scribbling when I am in a hurry, I would save myself from inconveniencing other people. It's I who must apologize."

"Not at all," he said a trifle automatically.

"You're very kind." She looked through the windows at the lawn and the carefully planned curved walk, which appeared to lead to spaces beyond but in reality probably doubled back on itself. "It does not look too windy out there, and it certainly is not raining. Would you be gracious enough to show me around the garden? I think it has a remarkable art to it, which I find most pleasing."

He could hardly refuse. "Of course," he said reluctantly. His body was tense and his hands oddly stiff as he walked over to the door and opened it for her.

As they crossed the terrace and went down the steps, she began the conversation for which she had come.

"I recently had a most delightful visit with Alphonsine Gifford, and she told me of your forthcoming engagement. May I congratulate you? She is in every way a charming young woman."

"Thank you." The shadow of a smile softened his face, but he did not turn his head or meet her eyes.

"It will be good to have someone to stand by you and be of support should this wretched business of Tregarron come to trial," she went on. "It cannot be pleasant to have to testify to such a distressing incident."

He stopped on the edge of the grass. "I don't think I shall have to do that. Surely the evidence is perfectly plain? I . . . I didn't really do anything."

"All the more reason why you should testify, if he is found," she said gently. "You will have had a clearer view and, I daresay, a clearer head. You seemed to me to be a little more . . . sober . . . than the others."

He gasped, and she realized that

perhaps he had forgotten for a moment that she had been there, moments after the incident, when Tregarron was still attempting to revive Winnie and the other three young men were standing close by.

She waited for him to continue. The silence was heavy and awkward.

He started to speak and then changed his mind.

She was acutely aware of his difficulty, but she could not afford to break the silence or change the subject, as she would have at any other time.

"It was all . . . ridiculous and unpleasant," he said at last. "Tregarron should never have been invited. He's a complete outsider . . . appalling man. Creighton can't possibly have known how he would behave, or he wouldn't have had anything to do with him."

"Creighton Foxley invited him?" She affected surprise. She really only wanted to get a response from him.

"Well . . . I . . ." He trailed off unhappily.

"You are very loyal." The remark was not complimentary. Her voice held a shadow of the contempt she felt for his seeming emotional indifference to the tragedy of a young woman's death and the fact that neither he nor his friends had done anything effective to prevent it.

Ernest blushed hotly. "Yes, I am, Mrs. Burroughs. I have no intention of discussing the matter unless I am forced to. But of course I will testify against Tregarron, if they call me. I'm angry that the man was allowed onto the premises, especially into Miss Gifford's home. But when we are married I shall make certain that such a thing doesn't happen again."

"Of course," Claudine agreed, her heart sinking as she pictured a long and fiercely protected life stretching ahead for Alphonsine. Was it what she wanted? Or what she believed it wise to settle for? Perhaps there were sides to Ernest Halversgate that Claudine had failed to see. "I'm sure you will find it distasteful to stand in court and tell the public exactly what happened," she said more soothingly than she felt. "Any of us would. But you are, above all, a man of honor, so that is what you will do. I am so sorry any of this happened."

He managed a bleak smile then moved forward and pointed out a particularly fine holly bush that was brilliant with berries.

"Superb," she murmured politely but quite honestly. "Holly is such good value, I think. It provides color, shape, and interest in a garden when there is so little else at this time of year."

They made meaningless conversation around the rest of the garden, which was not nearly as large as clever optical illusion had suggested.

At last they reached the door to the withdrawing room again. Tolly Halversgate was standing just inside, controlling her expression of annoyance with some difficulty.

"I'm so sorry," she said coolly. "I thought I had made my arrangement clear, but apparently I was remiss. I hope Ernest kept you entertained." There was no lift in her voice to make it a question. She was expressing criticism, not concern. She glanced at her son with anxiety. He met her eyes then looked away.

"He was charming," Claudine said with warmth. "What a perfectly delightful garden you have. In this mild weather he was kind enough to show me some of its very

best aspects. It seems his grandfather had a gift for design that I
very much admire."

Tolly's eyebrows rose in something that looked like disbelief. "I
had no idea you were interested in
garden design."

"Surely anything that creates
beauty is interesting?" Claudine
countered.

"Tea?" Tolly asked. Then before
Claudine could reply, she turned
to her son. "Thank you, Ernest.
Please feel now that you may leave
to continue with your own business. I'm sure Mrs. Burroughs will
excuse you, and I am most obliged
for your courtesy."

"Thank you for your company,
and your conversation, Mr. Hal-

versgate," Claudine said courteously.

"My pleasure." He bowed in a stiff and rather old-fashioned manner for such a young man. Then, without adding anything further, he left the room.

"What an agreeable and sensitive person he is," Claudine said approvingly as she sat down in the chair by the fire, opposite the one nearest Tolly. "So much more mature than others I meet who are his age."

Tolly stared at her.

Claudine continued to smile, feeling as if she were baring her teeth. "Miss Gifford must be very happy, and quite confident in her future."

"We have not announced their

engagement yet," Tolly said a trifle sharply. However, her shoulders were relaxing a little, and there was a hint of satisfaction in her voice.

"Alphonsine told me herself." Claudine stretched the truth considerably. "Of course it is very difficult for a young woman to keep such secrets, especially when we are all involved in this other most unhappy matter." It was clumsy, but she could not think of a more tactful way to introduce the subject.

Tolly did not need to ask to which matter Claudine was referring. "I have no idea what you mean," she said coldly. "Ernest is not involved in it at all. He simply was unfortunate enough to have been close by, and he very naturally tried to restrain Tregarron. Heaven only knows what the other two were doing, inviting that man to the house in the first place. But if you had really thought about it, you would have realized that yourself." She looked at Claudine directly. "Naturally you were upset, having arrived at the scene before anyone else. Anybody would be. But if you look at it with hindsight, it is perfectly apparent what occurred."

Claudine looked at her with interest. Her mind was whirling, and there was a prickle of excitement stirring inside her: fear mixed with the scent of the hunt. She felt there was suddenly a glimpse of truth to be found here, beyond the carefully prepared words that had been there before.

"Yes. I am still thinking back over everything I saw," she answered, her own gaze not wavering from Tolly's.

"How wise of you," Tolly replied. "I can see that you are weighing your position very cautiously. After all, a word misplaced can do a lot of damage."

"It often can," Claudine agreed. "And once spoken, be very difficult to retract." She wondered if Tolly was merely concerned about her son's forthcoming engagement, which might be jeopardized if he appeared to be too closely involved with Tregarron. Or of the considerable unpleasantness if he were to testify in a way that reflected badly on Creighton Foxley and Cecil Crostwick, who were unquestionably leaders in their social set. Or possibly of the damage to Alphonsine's value if someone were to suggest, even obliquely, that Forbes Gifford's parties were of a character where men and women such as Tregarron and Winnie Briggs were often found.

Tolly smiled. "I see you understand exactly." Her voice was cold and careful. "I'm sure you will do the right thing. Alphonsine is a lovely young woman. My son is very fortunate. He will be marrying into a family who will take the greatest care of their daughter's reputation so neither of them will ever have cause for embarrassment.

I'm certain, had you a son, you would wish the same for him." Her smile grew wider, easier. "You understand the nuances precisely. Now, may I offer you tea? I'm sure after your walk you would like some refreshment."

"How kind of you," Claudine accepted, her mind racing to weigh all that Tolly's remarks were intended to mean. The Giffords were powerful, wealthy, quite capable either of helping Wallace in his climb to success or of hurting him. It would depend on Claudine's behavior regarding the situation and the reputations of everyone involved — not only Alphonsine's but, by implication, that of the young man she was going to marry.

If Claudine were to cause any kind of embarrassment, Tolly Halversgate would make very sure that she paid for it dearly.

Did that mean that there was some way in which Ernest Halversgate needed protection? Surely it did. Tolly was worried, and Ernest himself was afraid, afraid of his new friends, the circle of which he was on the edge and so badly wanted to be within. What price would he pay for that privilege? Telling lies as to who was responsible for Winnie Briggs's death? Would he let an innocent man hang for it?

If that was the case, Claudine must find a way to make sure he understood that price and that he would ultimately find it more than he was willing to pay.

Could she use Alphonsine some-how? How much of the truth did the girl know, or guess? Did Ernest know the answer to that, and did he care?

She could not yet answer those questions. Maybe it depended on whether Squeaky could confirm in any detail what Arthur Davidson had told her.

She remained talking idle non-sense to Tolly Halversgate until good manners were satisfied then took her leave.

Outside in the fresh air she walked briskly, her mind crowded with thoughts. The police might catch Dai Tregarron any day, unless of course he had left the country and gone overseas. The thought of him in another country, no matter how civilized or how beautiful, made her sad. She pictured an exile's loneliness, the rootless unbelonging of a man whose art was inspired by the land he loved.

She shook herself out of such useless speculation. She had spoken to him exactly twice, but his bruised and troubled face haunted her mind, making her behave like a stupid girl. She still hadn't confirmed that he wasn't guilty, and she needed to remember that and conduct her inquiries accordingly. Collect the facts, then deduce a theory to fit them — don't invent your theory then select your facts to suit. Hopefully, Squeaky could locate Tregarron and hear his side of the events. In the meantime, she must work with what she had. Begin again at the beginning.

She was obliged to find Oona Gifford at an early evening soirée. An exceptionally large soprano was giving a recital of songs celebrating Christmas in different languages. Donations were to be given to charities in aid of the unfortunate.

She had not intended to attend; it was a last resort in order to find Oona. As such, Claudine arrived late and was obliged to sit in the back row. That turned out to be a blessing, since from there she could see everyone else, and in the intermission Oona would be obliged to pass by her if she wished to leave for the refreshments. Considering the seriousness and the monotony of the songs, that was extremely likely. Claudine herself would certainly leave and do everything within her power to avoid being invited to meet the hostess, or anyone else for whom she would have to invent a flattering opinion. It would be comparatively easier to part with a suitable financial offering.

In the end, Oona saw Claudine before Claudine saw her.

"Thank goodness!" Oona said with intense relief. "Please say you have something urgent to discuss with me and we must do it alone, because it would be most ill-mannered to disturb other people's listening enjoyment by making a noise. We must find somewhere private . . . as soon as possible. My head is ringing from these high notes. I'm not sure I shall ever hear a top C again without ducking in case the chandeliers shatter in pieces."

Claudine did not bother to hide her pleasure, even if she made a rather poor attempt to disguise it as surprise.

"How fortunate I am to see you," she said, quite seriously. "I'm afraid I must ask you to interrupt your enjoyment and spare me time to speak with you a little more privately. Most inconsiderate of me, I know, but it really does matter."

Oona looked taken aback. She searched Claudine's face for sarcasm and found none.

"I'm perfectly serious," Claudine assured her. "Seeing you is actually the reason I came. You didn't think I came for the music, did you?" She made the tone light and her smile a little rueful. She liked Oona, and being candid was not difficult, only a little uncomfortable in that she did not wish to hurt her.

Oona held out her hand in a gesture of invitation. "Then let us find somewhere uninterrupted and discuss whatever it is you wish." She turned and led the way out of the gallery and up a flight of steps to a landing out of sight from the main hall.

"What's happened?" she asked when they faced each other. "Not something more to do with Tregarron, is it? I really don't know who invited him. It certainly was not I. I suspect it might have been Creighton Foxley."

"It is to do with Tregarron, one way or another," Claudine admitted, trying to get her thoughts in order. She had expected to have to work her way toward candor, not be pitched headfirst into it at the moment of meeting. Now her careful plans were completely overturned. "I had a delightful meeting with Alphonsine the other day," she continued after a pause. "She told me she is shortly to become engaged to Ernest Halversgate." She let the statement hang in the air as if it were a question. She studied Oona's face as she framed her reply. She saw anxiety in it and a degree of uncertainty. It mirrored her own feelings exactly.

Oona was extraordinarily candid, more than any other woman in Claudine's acquaintance would have been. "Do you know something about Ernest Halversgate that you think perhaps I don't?" she asked.

Claudine replied with another question. She was surprised how much she cared that Oona should think well of her, or at the very least know that she spoke out of honesty and concern, not unkindness.

"Do you know Mr. Halversgate

very well?"

"No. Alphonsine is my stepdaughter. This arrangement has been made by her father, and I do not believe it is my place to question his judgment — even had I any cause to." She frowned, the concern in her face deepening. "Are you suggesting that there is some reason why I should?"

"I know nothing ill of him," Claudine assured her. "Except perhaps he is a tad unwise in the company he keeps. But it might be prudent to delay the announcement until there is more of a resolution to the death of that unfortunate young woman. I . . . I appreciate that it would be loyal to express your confidence in him, publicly, but perhaps be certain beforehand that that is what Alphonsine herself wishes. I may be speaking quite out of turn." She felt the hot color burn up her face. It was more than out of turn; it was meddlesome and possibly quite unjust. But Mr. Davidson's information was too serious to ignore, for Alphonsine's sake, quite apart from the need to know the truth about Winnie Briggs's death.

Oona was regarding her intently. "Are you carefully avoiding saying that you think there is something in Ernest Halversgate's behavior that we would find more than youthful indiscretion? Please be honest. Alphonsine is not my daughter, but I love her as dearly as if she were." She took a deep breath. "Ernest is not my choice, he is her father's, made with every consideration for her happiness. Ernest has an excellent reputation, both for sobriety and for wisdom, and the considerable ability to handle money well. Alphonsine will have a very large inheritance, eventually. She is an only child, and my husband loves her deeply."

"I can understand that it is a fundamental consideration that she marry a man who is both honest and prudent," Claudine agreed. The fact that Wallace Burroughs was both these things loomed in her mind.

"I hear no enthusiasm in your voice," Oona said unhappily. "Alphonsine is being very . . . awkward about it herself. I had attributed it to the fact that Ernest is — to put it frankly — dull. When we are young we look for romance, excitement, even a little danger. Only when we have tasted those qualities and find they leave a bitter taste, do we see the beauty of reliability, and of kindness, if you like."

Claudine closed her eyes for a moment, swallowing hard, then opened them again. "The voice of wisdom," she said in little more than a whisper. "But I notice you make kindness important. Real kindness has its roots in strength, don't you think? Without it, and courage, when would his apparent kindness become merely good intentions, which at the slightest chill can wither into nothing?"

Oona blinked several times, her face bleak with anxiety.

"I have the strongest feeling that you are trying to warn me against something, but I cannot see what. I know already that Alphonsine does not love Ernest, and I am not at all sure whether he loves her or not. But at twenty who knows the difference between love and infatuation? I have been infatuated a few times, haven't you?"

"Yes," Claudine agreed ruefully. The memory brought sudden pain, not of grief but of embarrassment.

Oona was smiling. "I see your choices were no wiser than mine. My parents decided my first marriage, and I know they meant well. He was much older than I, and he died quite early, leaving me free to choose my own second marriage. I am fortunate enough to be very happy in that. Enough that I will not impose my advice over his when it comes to a husband for his daughter, even if I might find poor Ernest both pompous and with little passion or humor." She gave a slight shrug. "But then, I liked Mr. Tregarron, so what does that say for my judgment?"

"I liked him, too," Claudine admitted. "But I would not let my daughter marry him, had I a daughter."

"Would you let her marry Ernest Halversgate? And please, do answer that honestly, or not at all."

"Not until the death of Winnie Briggs has been resolved more fully," Claudine said gravely.

"I see." Oona nodded. "Yes, I think I do see. Perhaps Alphonsine's reluctance to obey her father's wish in the matter should be considered more seriously. She loves him very much and would not be awkward just on a whim. I think I shall try to persuade him that after this recent unpleasantness, she should be given rather more time. He thinks women are fragile." She smiled with a sudden bright tenderness. "Which is utter nonsense, of course, but on this occasion I might pretend that I agree with him. Thank you. This cannot have been easy for you to say."

Claudine smiled back at her. "Easier than listening to the rest of the songs," she said lightly. They both laughed with fellowship, and there was a sudden easing of the tension.

Claudine went to the clinic the next day, determined to coerce Squeaky into further action regarding Winnie Briggs, even if it meant taking over some of the bookkeeping herself. The weather was still mild, but it was raining. She was glad to be inside where she could take off her wet boots and put on dry ones.

She intended to remain only until she could speak with Squeaky and find out if he had learned anything further. Regardless of what he said, she must tell him of her growing conviction that Ernest Halversgate was lying about something, and perhaps Alphonsine was, too. Might he even have confided in her? Or possibly she had guessed as much from his manner, or a slip of the tongue?

Claudine worked for nearly two hours, mostly on arrangements to provide a really good Christmas dinner for any patients who were resident in the clinic or who might come in longing for a dry bed and a warm roof over their heads on the days that were set aside to celebrate the birth of Christ, and the charity that went with that event. Efforts to ease the longing for a sign there was an eternity beyond the grief of this world, where so many had so little chance of happiness.

It was almost midday when Squeaky staggered in, disheveled and bleary-eyed. He led the way to his office and sat down heavily in his chair. Claudine looked at him. Both compassion and practicality sent her away immediately to fetch him a pot of tea and several slices of toast. She set them down in front of him and then took the chair opposite the desk and demanded his attention.

"Take your breakfast," she ordered him brusquely. "Eat the toast, whether you feel like it or not, and drink two cups of tea. I shall tell you what I have learned.

Then, when you have finished and feel fit to conduct yourself like a man, you will tell me what you have learned."

For once he did not argue. It was only too clear that he had spent a long and supremely testing night, and much of it had been unpleasant. She wished to know exactly where he had been and what he had learned and did not intend to allow him to evade answering.

Carefully she recounted to him whom she had seen and all that had been said that mattered. She had brought two cups on the tray, and had tea herself, then wished she had also brought more toast. He ate all five slices himself, with butter and marmalade.

"Well?" she said impatiently when he had swallowed the last mouthful.

He shook his head slowly, pursing his lips. "Foxley and Crostwick are two very self-indulgent young men," he said, framing the words carefully, his eyes on hers to watch her reaction.

"Self-indulgent," she repeated. "Don't wrap it up, Squeaky. We don't have time."

"Couple o' drunken sods." He relaxed a little. "Bullies, lechers, arrogant bastards, but with enough money, and charm when they need it, so's they get away with it. You won't get anybody to swear to it — not that they'd be believed anyway. Can see how they get along with

Dai Tregarron. Natural companion, you might say. Except that he can hold his drink better, and charm the women so as he don't have to pay nobody."

"But not Ernest Halversgate?" she pressed. Squeaky had confirmed what Arthur Davidson had said.

"Not him." Squeaky lifted his shoulders exaggeratedly. "Much too tight-collared and stiff-necked to do that sort of thing. Wants to be one of the boys, but only to be included, not for its own sake. Too careful, too clean." He raised his hands dramatically, the gesture losing something because of the ink stains on his fingers.

"By nature or out of fear?" she

asked.

"Ah," he sighed. "Clever. I don't know. Does she have a lot of money, this Miss Gifford?"

"She will do," Claudine answered. "Why? Do you think he's careful because he wants to be master of that? Forbes Gifford has a deep affection for his daughter. And so, actually, does her stepmother. If anything really unsavory were known about Ernest, I am sure the engagement would not go ahead. Actually —" She stopped, not sure what she wanted to say, or if it should be said to Squeaky Robinson.

"What?" he demanded.

She should trust him. She had asked for his help without offering any reward to him for his trouble, only perhaps discomfort, even danger.

"I think Alphonsine herself is not entirely happy with the prospect of marrying Ernest Halversgate," she answered. "But I don't know the reason. Possibly she has learned something that her parents don't know, but she might not be able to prove it . . . Or maybe she heard it in confidence and cannot repeat it without betraying whoever it is that told her."

Squeaky shook his head. "Comes of having nothing else to worry about," he observed.

"What does?" She was confused.

"Gentry," he replied patiently. "Makes life a whole lot more complicated than it has to be. Don't just marry someone you want to marry, follow all these complicated rules — it's like learning the steps of a dance. Never go to anything in a straight line, stop and twirl and twiddle all over the place before you finally get where you're trying to go, when a plain man would've simply taken a couple of strides, following his nose. Still, got to have something to do with your time, I s'pose."

"It's not to do with time, Squeaky," she said. "It's to do with separating the best people from the second best."

"Best?" he retorted indignantly. "In whose eyes?"

"Their own, of course. Do you

think they even know there is any-body else?" She smiled as she said it, but there was a hard, sad honesty underneath the humor.

He stared at her. "You're an odd one, Mrs. B. Lot more to you than meets the eye, an' that's the truth."

"I think I had better see Alphon-sine again," she said. "What will you do?"

"Balance the bleedin' books," Squeaky said tartly. "Then maybe I'll go and look some more for Tre-garron." Suddenly he was deeply serious. "If I find him, do you think I should tell him to get the hell out of England? They'll hang him, you know."

"Yes, of course I do." She heard her own voice tight and hard in her throat. "I don't know the answer. If he goes, he'll never face trial, so in other people's eyes he'll always be guilty. It'll mean he can't ever come home again. That would matter more to him than to some men."

Squeaky raised his eyebrows.

"I've read some of his poetry," she said abruptly. "And that's another thing. His life as a poet, and his reputation, matter to him."

"Well. If I tell 'im to stay, you'd better be right," he said grimly. "There isn't going to be no second shots at it!"

"I know. If you do find him, speak to him honestly." She took a deep breath. "And we should face the possibility that he really did kill her, even if he didn't mean to."

He grunted. "Judge ain't going to make no distinction," he pointed out. "If he were Cecil Crostwick, for instance, the judge might say it was all an unfortunate accident, and we'll treat it like a brawl that went wrong. But the powers that be'll make damn sure with Dai Tregarron that they swing him by the neck. He in't one of *them.* In fact, he's rather gone out of his way, one time and another, to make a point of that."

"I know. You might remind him of that, too, if you do find him."

Squeaky shrugged and picked up the teapot to see if there was anything left in it. He put it down again, disappointed. "Not much chance of it. If he's any sense, he'll be in Timbuktu by now." He frowned. "I s'pose I get to go back out again!"

"We also need to find a connection between Briggs and Foxley or Crostwick," she pointed out.

He glared at her and sighed heavily, but stood up again and pulled his coat back onto his shoulders.

Again it required a little engineering and quite a lot of duplicity from Claudine to arrange to meet with Alphonsine alone.

She regretted it, but time was short. If Claudine was right about the boys being guilty, then Alphonsine might suffer dearly in the years to come through her marriage to

Ernest. And Dai Tregarron might pay with his life.

Was she fueled by a need for justice, righteous indignation, or just plain, ordinary anger? She did not yet have an answer for that question.

The place she expected to encounter Alphonsine was an exhibition of archaeological pieces recently found in Asia Minor. She was beginning to think all her elaborate plotting was for nothing when she finally saw the young woman standing alone in front of a display of glass jewelry, seeming to be deep in thought.

Claudine knew she was intruding. It made her hesitate a moment and then carry on regardless. An afternoon's unwelcome clumsiness was little enough compared with the misery that would follow if she was right, and did nothing.

"How pleasant to see you, Miss Gifford," Claudine said warmly, even though she kept her voice low. "This display gives one a whole new perception of the period, doesn't it?"

Alphonsine was startled, and she did not have the presence of mind to keep her dismay from her face.

Claudine decided for complete candor, then. "I am aware that I am interrupting you when you would prefer to be alone," she admitted. "If the matter could have waited, I assure you, I would have left you in peace. My interest in history is not so obsessive as to compel me to share it with someone. I am much more concerned with the recent past, and the near future."

Alphonsine scrambled to be courteous. "I don't think I understand you, Mrs. Burroughs. But it is most pleasant to see you. If I looked otherwise, it was merely because I was startled out of my reverie."

"You are very generous," Claudine responded. "But I can see that you are troubled and wish to be left in peace. Unfortunately, time and events will not wait for us."

Alphonsine pretended for a moment that she did not understand. Then, meeting Claudine's eyes, she knew that the struggle was destined to fail.

"Earlier you seemed confident that Mr. Halversgate did not have anything to do with the death of Winnie Briggs. That it was simply a case of being at the wrong place at the crucial time," Claudine began.

"Yes, yes, that's quite right," Alphonsine agreed quickly. "He tried to help, but as we all know, it was too late by then." She looked away.

Claudine thought of the lies Alphonsine had purportedly connived at in order to spend more time with Ernest.

"You care for him very much . . . ," she said aloud.

Alphonsine looked confused. For a moment her face betrayed the absurdity of the idea, then she masked it quickly.

"Of course," she replied.

"No one has been very clear as to how it began," Claudine went on. She kept her voice low and quite casual, as if she were actually discussing the old, rather dented beads in front of them, which might have been worn by a woman three thousand years ago, under a hot Middle Eastern sun. And here were they, two English women with fair skins wrapped up against the English winter, staring at them and talking about anger, fear, and murder.

"How little changes," she said aloud.

Alphonsine turned toward her, the question in her face.

"The necklace," Claudine replied,

glancing at the beads. "I wonder what she was like, the woman who wore those. Who gave them to her? More important, I wonder if he loved her." Claudine voiced her thoughts. She had never been beautiful — she had known that from the start — but she would like to have been loved, above all things. She would have to settle for being liked, perhaps for being trusted, respected. Best of all would have been to have had the courage to stand up for herself and fight for what she believed in.

Alphonsine was looking at the beads again. "I wonder if she was happy."

Claudine heard the pain in her voice — or perhaps "wistfulness"

would be a more accurate word —
and knew with sudden clarity that
Alphonsine's stolen time was not
spent with Ernest Halversgate. She
was reveling in her freedom, while
she still had it. Maybe she had
come here to be alone, to indulge
in her dreams while she could,
before they were marred by an inner sense of having betrayed herself.

Claudine tried to put her own
feelings aside. "There are many
kinds of happiness, some of them
within our reach, regardless of
circumstances," she said. "How
much of the truth do you know of
that evening, Alphonsine? Was it
really Dai Tregarron who beat Winnie Briggs? Or was it a more general

fight that simply got out of hand?"

Alphonsine looked away. "Why do you think I know?"

"Because of what you have already told me," Claudine replied. "You are afraid that if Ernest Halversgate is called to testify, he will say something that shouldn't be said. I don't know whether that is because he will tell some truth that is inconsistent with what has been told to the police, or if you are afraid that he will lie, and very possibly be caught in that lie, becoming a suspect himself." She saw the fear crystallize in Alphonsine's eyes. "Or else that he will not be caught," she added, "but will cause the blame to fall on someone else, and in so doing see an innocent man hanged, and the rest of your own lives are then destroyed from within. And they will be. Never doubt that."

Alphonsine's eyes brimmed with tears.

"You have the chance to act now," Claudine said gently. "Perhaps you are wise enough to imagine what the future will be, whereas the young men concerned are not. They are afraid. That is easy to understand. So are you. It is there, very easy to read in your eyes. If they have neither the courage nor the honor to act for themselves, then you must do it for Tregarron. If you don't, and he is hanged wrongly, do you not think you will be haunted by his face and theirs, and imagine a rope around your own neck every time you lie alone in the dark, for the rest of your life?"

Alphonsine said nothing for a long time. Then at last she spoke.

"It was all fairly good-natured to begin with," she said quietly. "Then they got a bit insistent, demanding that Winnie . . . do more and more. She refused. It got a bit rough. I don't remember who it was. There's no good pushing me because I didn't see. She slapped him. He lost his temper. Then it got really rough. Someone hit her, and she fell against Ernest. I saw that."

"They were all on the terrace?" Claudine interrupted, trying to visualize it in her mind.

"Yes. Tregarron was a bit apart from the others, a bit farther away. They were moving about, pushing and shoving, you know?"

"I can picture it. Then what happened?"

"Ernest . . . Ernest was angry. I think someone must've broken a glass and spilled their drink over him."

"You smelled it . . . afterward?" Claudine interrupted quickly.

Alphonsine turned away again. "Yes."

"Then what?"

"I . . . I didn't see clearly. There was more pushing and a few blows. Someone shoved Winnie very hard, and she fell down completely. She was angry then, and when she got up she lashed back at someone. I only saw her arm swing. And there was blood. I mean, I don't know who she struck. But whoever it was, he struck back very hard. That was when I saw Dai Tregarron lunge forward at him and punch him, but he missed his face and caught his shoulder. The two of them fought, just a few blows. Tregarron staggered against the pillar. I think it was then that they realized Winnie was on the ground, and she wasn't moving."

"Who had hit her, Alphonsine?"

"I don't know. Except it wasn't Mr. Tregarron. Then he was bent over trying to get his breath, leaning against the pillar, when he saw she was on the ground, just lying there. He tried to help her. That was when you came in."

Claudine stared at her, stunned, her mind racing.

"I swear, that is the truth," Alphonsine said urgently.

"Part of it, anyway," Claudine agreed. "You don't know who it was who hit Winnie Briggs hard enough to kill her, when she fell and her head struck the ground. But you do know it wasn't Dai Tregarron. You know that if they catch him they will try him for murder, and if they find him guilty — and without your story there is no reason why they wouldn't — then they will hang him?"

Alphonsine gulped air and nearly choked. "Yes . . ." It was a whisper.

"But I can't prove it, and they will only say that I'm lying. I — I can't prove it . . . I really can't!"

"You were there!" Claudine protested.

Alphonsine stared at her. Claudine thought back to the night: the terrace, Winnie lying on the stones, her face white, not moving. She remembered Dai Tregarron's black head bent as he tried to revive her, and Cecil Crostwick, Creighton Foxley, and Ernest Halversgate standing pale and shivering nearby. She did not remember seeing Alphonsine anywhere.

And yet Alphonsine had just described the incident in some detail, exactly as if she had seen it: confusion, anger, stupidity, and a fatal mistake.

"Where were you?" Claudine asked quietly.

"I . . . I was in the morning room. It looks out onto the terrace."

"I see. Thank you." Claudine smiled. "I'm sorry to have been so persistent."

Alphonsine relaxed a little and looked away. "It's all right. I understand."

Claudine took her leave and caught a hansom toward her home again. She relaxed against the cushion, tired and relieved, thinking over what Alphonsine had said. Her testimony, however reluctantly given, would show Tregarron's innocence. Should she have asked the girl what she had been doing in the morning room, or was that irrelevant? Speaking to someone? Avoiding someone! Staring out of the window at the terrace? And why had she been so slow to come forward? Because it implicated Halversgate; that was the obvious answer. Then Claudine had a cold thought: perhaps because it was less than the whole truth, after all?

With a weariness that reached her very bones, Claudine leaned forward and very unwillingly instructed the driver to take her to the Giffords' house. At this time of the day, it was quite possible no one would be at home. It should not be too difficult to gain a few moments alone in the morning room. The servants would merely think her very eccentric. Perhaps they did anyway. It was not an excuse to avoid doing what she must.

Half an hour later she returned to the exhibition. She walked all the way through it until she came to the tearoom and found Alphonsine sitting at one of the small tables with a friend. She glanced up and saw Claudine. Her hand froze in the air, her cup halfway to her lips.

Claudine stopped, still gazing at Alphonsine.

Alphonsine lowered her cup and rose to her feet. She said something to her friend then walked over toward Claudine.

"Please . . . not here . . . ," she

pleaded earnestly. Her eyes were wide, filled with fear.

"You were not in the morning room," Claudine said very quietly. "If what you said you saw is the truth — and I believe it is — then you must have been much farther around the terrace. You must've been in the house next door. That was how you saw what happened, but only partially. And that was why none of them saw you."

Alphonsine was very pale. She was trembling.

At last the pieces fell into place, and Claudine understood.

"This is why you do not wish to marry Ernest Halversgate, isn't it?" she asked. "It has to be. There is someone else."

The tears slid down Alphonsine's cheeks. "My father won't ever permit it. He wouldn't even consider it."

"I assume he is unsuitable?" Claudine understood perfectly. They belonged to the same world. If it was a young man with no prospects, or perhaps a youngest son, he would be unacceptable, neighbor or not. Claudine had once dreamed a similar dream and then given it up to obey her father's wishes. She had no idea whether it would ever have worked well, or even at all. At her father's insistence, the young man had never given her the chance to accept, or himself the chance to be refused.

She had not remembered it so

vividly for years. Now she understood far better than Alphonsine
could imagine.

"It's hard, I know," she said gently. "But what happiness is there
for you if you do not tell the truth
about this? You can convince your
parents, or the police, that you do
not know what happened. But can
you lie to yourself? You could avoid
going to Tregarron's trial, quite easily. In fact, it would be more difficult for you to go than not to. But
is that who you wish to be?"

"I can't tell them!" Alphonsine
said desperately. "It was an — an
assignation! If he knew of it, Ernest
would never have me! I didn't . . ."
She blushed scarlet.

"Of course you didn't," Claudine

agreed. "But you saw this young man alone, romantically, when you were supposed to be in your own house and engaged, at least in understanding, to Ernest. I do appreciate your situation. He is somewhat straitlaced, to put it kindly."

Alphonsine swallowed hard. "Very kindly. He bores me till I could weep!"

Claudine smiled at her with intense gentleness. "My dear, I do understand. Believe me, I do. But if they arrest Mr. Tregarron and charge him with murder, then you must speak. You have no choice."

"Please . . ."

"I will say nothing, unless I have to," Claudine promised. "But I will not let them blame an innocent man, or let go one who is guilty."

"I don't know which one of them is guilty! I really don't!"

"I know. But maybe we will be able to find out or prove it some other way."

"Do you think so?" Hope flared in Alphonsine's eyes.

"No," Claudine said honestly, "I don't."

Wallace Burroughs was in a good mood that evening over dinner. They had barely begun the soup when he told her the reason.

"The police have caught Tregarron," he said, smiling at her over the gleaming silver cruet sets and the sparkle of glasses.

Claudine put her soupspoon back

down in the plate. Her hand was shaking so much that he would have noticed.

"Really?" Her mouth was dry. The word sounded forced. "That was very efficient of them." She swallowed. "Where?"

"In Dover. Trying to escape, I suppose. I'm glad you're taking it so sensibly," he observed. "I was afraid you might be upset."

He seemed to be waiting for her to say something.

"Were you?" she replied. "I think it was inevitable, wasn't it?"

"Of course, since he left too late. He could have gone earlier. People like him always think they're invulnerable."

"People like him?" she questioned

then instantly wished she had not. It would only provoke a quarrel. She did not want to hear his opinion of Tregarron, and she had just been stupid enough to invite it.

"Drunkards," he replied. "Lechers, men who imagine that whatever talent they possess puts them above the laws that apply to ordinary people. Well, he'll discover he's wrong. Thank heaven it happened before Christmas, and it won't cloud the whole season for us. You should be glad it's over with."

"It isn't 'over with,'" she argued instantly. "They'll have to try him. We can't execute people just because we don't approve of them, or because they drink too much. Fortunately for a great many in our aristocratic class, drinking to excess is not a crime at all, let alone a capital one."

"Gentlemen know how to hold their drink," he said tartly.

"Oh, Wallace, don't be absurd!" she said with something close to a guffaw. "We just pretend we haven't noticed when they can't. I've picked up my skirts and walked around enough 'gentlemen' lying in the gutter not to have many illusions left."

He glared at her. "They may not stay upright on their feet, but they do not murder harlots on the terrace, Claudine. There is a difference."

She raised her eyebrows.

"A difference between the terrace and some back alley? A geographical one. It seems to be a distinction rather than a difference. I'm sure the harlot would rather prefer not to be attacked at all. The location of it probably matters very little to her."

"Claudine, your language has become very coarse lately. I don't care for the effect on you that working at the clinic seems to be having. Perhaps it would be better if you were to desist for a while. A year or two, maybe."

She did not retreat as usual, even though she knew she was losing, and would continue to do so. She looked at him inquiringly. "Is 'harlot' an unfortunate word? I learned it from you, Wallace. You used it just now, at the dinner table. I assure you I did not hear it at the clinic. It is not a term we use there. It is unnecessarily insulting."

His face burned hot, but with anger rather than embarrassment. "Well, did you learn your insolence there? I assure you that you did not get that from me," he snapped back, mimicking her tone.

"Of course not," she agreed. "You have no one to be insolent toward. Just as your employees dare not be insolent to you, out of fear of losing their positions, you are not insolent to your superiors, or you would lose yours."

He pushed his soup plate away from him, empty. He had not

stopped eating while speaking to her. "They will try Tregarron in the New Year," he said, ignoring her statement. "I imagine he will be hanged before the end of January. Damn good thing, too. He is a bad influence all round."

"I agree with you." She pushed her plate away also, although it was barely touched. "He seems to have had a profound effect on Creighton Foxley and on Cecil Crostwick. How sad that they will have to find harlots on their own now. Oh, I'm sorry. You don't like that word. I'm not sure I can think of another that quite fits the circumstances."

"Was there wine in the soup?" he said patronizingly.

"I have no idea. Do you wish for

some?"

"It seems you have had more than enough. Did you already know that Tregarron had been arrested?"

"No. I had no idea. And I have had no wine at all. Would you be kind enough to ring the bell for the butler? I have eaten sufficiently. Perhaps he would bring the next course."

From there, the evening became worse, as she had known it would.

"They won't try Tregarron over Christmas, but they'll likely do it straight afterward. If only to get it out of the way." Squeaky sat across from her at his desk in the clinic, gritting his teeth. It was now five days before Christmas. The weather was still mild. There was no frost in the air, no ice on the ground. "I wish the stupid sod had left the country." He gave a grunt of annoyance. "I should've found him. Got him to go. I'm no bloody use at all — I've lost my touch. That's respectability for you!"

His voice was so full of self-disgust that Claudine was momentarily sorry for him. "You learned quite a bit about his life," she pointed out.

He gave a bitter look. "That he wasn't seen hitting women. What good is that? You never thought he was guilty anyway."

"I didn't think so because I didn't want to," she said with rather more honesty than she had intended. She had not meant him to know that. "Now I know because of a pattern of behavior you have traced."

"Yeah? And what difference does that make? Who's going to believe the likes of you or me?"

Claudine was taken aback by the idea that her word was of no more credibility than that of an ex– brothel keeper, but Squeaky was probably right.

"Then we have to get Alphonsine to testify," she said firmly. She did not know what Squeaky would make of what she was about to tell him. "But it will be difficult, because she'll have to say where she was."

"What do you mean?" he demanded.

"She saw the whole thing. She knows that it wasn't Dai Tregarron who hit Winnie Briggs — but she doesn't know which of the young men it was."

He blinked. "How's that?"

"From where she was standing, she could see Tregarron; he was farther down the terrace, and when Winnie was hit, when he realized it had become ugly, he moved to stop it. But she was already down before he could do anything."

Squeaky was silent as he weighed her words. "You're certain?" he said finally.

"Yes, I am," Claudine assured him.

Squeaky nodded slowly. "That's a big step forward," he conceded with respect. "Now can we get her to admit that to the police? To say it in court, if it comes to that?"

"That might be difficult. You see, Alphonsine couldn't distinguish the other young men clearly, and none of them could see her, because she was across the terrace behind the windows of another house," she explained. "The lights on the terrace made them visible to her."

"Was she standing in the dark, then?"

"Yes. It . . . it was an assignation. She wasn't alone."

Squeaky turned that over in his mind for several moments. "Couldn't she just say that she was alone?"

Claudine looked at him witheringly. "Doing what?"

"What?" he asked.

"Why on earth would she be standing alone in the dark in a neighbor's house, staring out of the window at the terrace of her own house?" she said with as much patience as she could manage, which was very little indeed. Her voice sounded thin and tense.

He took the point and did not bother to say so. "And what would happen if she just plain told the truth?" he asked.

"It would jeopardize her engagement to Ernest Halversgate, because he would know that at the very best she did not love him, and at worst that she was actually involved with someone else. Knowing about it would be bad enough, but everyone else knowing would be unendurable. The arrangement would be ended."

"Didn't you say it hadn't even begun yet?" Squeaky looked at her sideways.

"Not formally," she agreed. "Informally, it is as if it were carved in stone."

"So he'll break it off — because she's betrayed him?" The ways of society still annoyed him. "Doesn't he love her?"

"I doubt it. But she will inherit a great deal of money, in due course."

"Well that's better than love. If he's got any bloody brains at all, he'll forgive her, from a great height, and keep the engagement,"

Squeaky said with conviction. "By the way — not that it matters, I suppose — but who *does* she love? Or would she rather not have either of them?"

"I think she would rather have the other one, but he has no money," Claudine replied.

"Is he any good?" He looked at her curiously.

"I don't know. Perhaps I should find out. But it will all depend upon her father anyway."

"Are you sure she's telling the truth?" He squinted at her a little sideways.

She was surprised. "Do you doubt it?"

"Well, she's kind of cornered, ain't she?" he pointed out. "Her father's got her into this arrangement, which she doesn't like, but she can't see her way out of it. Now suddenly she's got the chance to play a real blinder by saying she was with another man an' she saw this fight clearly enough to say Dai Tregarron wasn't guilty. And on her conscience she has to come forward and say so, even though it'll make her unwanted fiancé unwant her a great deal more. He'll break it off, and there'll be nothing she can do about it. Maybe she'll find that the only man who'll have her now is the one she wants anyway."

Claudine stared at him in growing horror.

"Better than that," Squeaky went on, "she can even realize, right at the last minute when she's been persuaded enough, that it were actually her fiancé that hit poor Winnie Briggs, and much as she hates doing it, honor forces her to testify to it."

It was a hideous scenario, and one that had not even occurred to Claudine. She struggled against it, trying to find even one reason why it could not be true. She failed. It could be exactly as Squeaky suggested.

In fact, the more she thought of it, the more she realized that Ernest Halversgate was going to be in trouble regardless, because he had clearly told the police that Winnie's assailant was Dai Tregarron. He had lied, either because he himself was actually involved or because he was prepared to send an innocent man to the gallows to save one of his guilty friends. That was, morally at least, also a kind of murder.

Squeaky was watching her, seeing in her face the thoughts reflected as they unfolded.

"Sorry," he said with a sudden gentleness. Then he looked away quickly.

Another, even worse thought occurred to her. What if, with her persistence, Claudine had unintentionally pushed Alphonsine into lying in the first place? Maybe Dai Tregarron was guilty, and by going on and on, insisting that there must be some other solution, she had maneuvered Alphonsine into this edifice of lies from which none of them would escape? What had her meddling done?

Wallace was right: She should have let the law take its course and kept well out of it. She had no skill, no knowledge, and very little sense. Suddenly, she was consumed with shame.

Squeaky was still watching her.

"What are you going to do?" he asked. It had clearly not occurred to him that she might do nothing.

"I don't know," she admitted.

"Well, you can't just sit there!" he exclaimed. "You done this — you'd better undo it."

She glared at him. She knew the truth; she did not need a semi-reformed brothel keeper, of all people, to tell her such things. Then she saw the concern in his face, which he probably had no idea he was betraying so openly; it caught her unawares, and she was quite painfully moved by it. He actually cared. It was an odd friendship — awkward, grown slowly from beginnings of mutual contempt — but it was real nonetheless.

She would not embarrass him by acknowledging it.

"I will go and face Alphonsine," she answered, "and persuade her to admit the truth, whatever that is. Perhaps we can even get this other young man to testify . . ."

The shadow cleared from Squeaky's face. "Well, you'd better get on then, hadn't you!" he said gruffly. "I got things to do, even if you haven't. I s'pose you haven't forgotten, but just in case you have, it's nearly Christmas."

Alphonsine did not seem surprised to see Claudine again. She arrived on what was ostensibly a Christmas call of general well-wishing, but both knew why she was truly there. They sat together in the morning room, as neither of them wished to be interrupted by others who might call. It was also a time of day when Oona would be out making her own visits.

"You will know that Mr. Tregarron has been arrested." Claudine did not waste time or stretch the tension unnecessarily by making light conversation about subjects neither of them cared about.

"Yes, my mother mentioned it," Alphonsine replied, looking down at the carpet. "I admit, I wondered if she knew anything about my . . . my knowledge of the incident. She brought it up most particularly."

"I daresay, she is anxious since the tragedy happened here at your house, and she can hardly be uninterested in the outcome," Claudine suggested.

"He'll be found guilty, and hanged," Alphonsine whispered. "You told me that. Unless I tell the police, and perhaps the court, that I saw what really happened and it was not Mr. Tregarron." She looked at Claudine like someone drown-

285

ing and already beyond reach of the shore.

"I'm afraid that as far as I can see, that is the truth," Claudine replied. "I wish I could think of an alternative, and I have tried."

"My father will be furious." Alphonsine still struggled. "He has been friends with the Halversgates for years."

"Yes, so I believe." Claudine made no allowances because of that fact. "I imagine he would not have liked you to marry into a family he did not know, and trust." She hoped Alphonsine would pick up the argument, if in fact she believed it could have been Ernest who struck Winnie. She searched Alphonsine's face to see if there was the duplicity in

it that Squeaky had imagined possible. She saw nothing but desperation for an escape, and rising panic.

"He'll despise me," Alphonsine
whispered.

"Your father or Ernest?" Claudine
asked her. It was important that she
did not misunderstand.

"Both . . . ," Alphonsine replied.

"Perhaps. But you surely know
that above whatever may happen,
your father loves you. And while
Ernest may not love you, you might
also consider that he was there on
the terrace at the time. He knows it
was not Dai Tregarron who killed
Winnie, and yet he is willing to allow him to be tried and hanged for
the crime. Is that because he is
guilty himself and wants to escape

the consequences? Or does he wish to protect one of his friends, friends who seem to matter more to him than honor or justice? Or is he afraid that if he speaks the truth, then there will be some price for him to pay in popularity? Does he fear for his safety, that if he speaks the truth, his friends will attack him and make him suffer for it in more personal and immediate ways? No matter which it is, does that seem like a man your father would wish you to marry and into whose hands he would place your future?"

"No! No, of course not." Alphonsine gave a bleak little smile. "But there are two things you have forgotten. One is that I was in the house next door with John before I knew of Ernest's weakness." She winced. And clearly not for the first time. "The other is that quite possibly no one will believe me, anyway. Creighton, Cecil, and Ernest will all say it was Tregarron in order to save themselves. And it is what everyone else will want to believe. It removes the matter from any of our hands. And can't you see what they will say of me? Isn't it obvious?"

Indeed it was obvious, and Claudine had already considered it. She knew what she was asking of Alphonsine. She would almost certainly lose the marriage prospect ahead of her. She would also gain the enmity of the Halversgates, not to mention the Foxleys and the

Crostwicks, whose sons' reputations she would drag into question. All of them had lied, but they would fight very hard to prove that it was Alphonsine who was the liar. They would paint her to be a loose and immoral young woman whose virtue was far from what she had claimed for it.

Silence would be so much easier. Everybody would approve of her. She would have a safe and prosperous marriage, her parents would be well satisfied, social events would proceed as before with nothing but an unpleasant incident clouding a few days before the Christmas celebrations wiped it away.

They would not even know what Alphonsine had done for them,

because the young men did not know she had witnessed the tragedy.

Even Dai Tregarron would not know that she could perhaps have saved him. He would not blame her.

Claudine herself would find it easier, in a way, to keep quiet. It would be more comfortable. Otherwise the young men's families would hate her, too, perhaps blame her the more, thinking her older and better able to foresee the grief Alphonsine's testimony would bring upon all of them. Wallace would be revoltingly self-satisfied. She could hear his voice in her head: *"I told you Tregarron was guilty! Why couldn't you see it, like everyone else?"*

Claudine looked again at the girl's face, the pain and the indecision in it, the increasing understanding of what speaking out would cost her. And she saw also a growing appreciation of what her silence would cost. Perhaps she glimpsed the long years ahead, of looking at Ernest Halversgate and knowing what he had done, that he would lie for his own comfort and see someone else hang for it.

Would she ever feel safe again? Might she let slip one day that she had seen what had happened? What then?

"Alphonsine," Claudine said gently, "I cannot tell you what you must do, but I can warn you as clearly as I am able to of what the price will be, whatever course you take."

Alphonsine looked at her, fear in her eyes, waiting.

"If you are certain of what you saw, I think you have no choice but to tell it now," Claudine said. "Or be prepared to live with your silence, and whatever consequences might follow it, for the rest of your life. You will presumably marry Ernest Halversgate, knowing that he also knows the truth and that he chose to remain silent. You had better be very sure that you never tell him you also know. As it stands, he will have to testify under oath. No one will ask you to testify because they do not know you saw anything.

Can you live with that silence, and do you trust the man you love, and who you were with, to keep that silence also? He knows you saw what happened. Possibly he saw it also. What manner of man is he?"

Alphonsine took a deep breath and let it out in a sigh. "He is an honest man," she whispered. "He will tell the truth. And he would despise me if I said nothing. The thought of that hurts more than I can bear. I have decided. Will you come with me?"

"Of course. Whom shall we see first?"

"John. His name is John Barton."

It was not quite so easy to arrange a meeting between Alphonsine and

John Barton, with Claudine present. It required a degree of subterfuge and rather a lot of hansom cab rides to one place and then another. Claudine did not dare take her own carriage. If Wallace were to ask the coachman where he had been all day that the horses were in such a lather, the reply would cause a good deal more trouble. Fortunately, she had funds to afford cab fares for both herself and Alphonsine.

Thus it was that late that evening they met with John Barton. He had excused himself from a dinner with his friends on the pretext of urgent business, the nature of which was private.

They found themselves walking

in the rain along the Mall, passing numbers of other people who were laughing and joking, putting up umbrellas and trying to keep them steady in the breeze.

"I'm sorry," Claudine said to John Barton, who was a very agreeable young man. He was not exactly handsome, but perhaps better than that — he had a face that showed both good humor and openness, coupled with a considerable intelligence. Had she been Alphonsine's age, Claudine had no doubt at all that she would have chosen him above Ernest Halversgate, whatever their difference in expectations or suitability.

But then Claudine was older and wiser. She had tasted years of pedestrian marriage that had now settled into a pattern of mutual dislike. If she had known then what she knew now, she would have taken the risks, sacrificed the parties, the balls, the theaters, the carriages, and the servants, in favor of a little hardship as the price of laughter and affection.

Not that she valued comfort lightly. It was easy to become used to, even to take for granted in a surprisingly short time. It was just that things had a different value when you were older and had lost the chance to make your decisions again.

"Mr. Barton," Claudine began as they moved down an empty pathway, the trees sheltering them from most of the damp. It was possible here to furl the umbrella again and speak more easily.

He turned to pay her his full attention.

Briefly she told him of their current situation regarding the struggle and death of Winnie Briggs and the fact that Tregarron was now in custody and due to be charged.

"I believe you and Alphonsine were in a situation where you witnessed at least a part of these unpleasant events." She made it more of a statement than a question, but she watched him carefully to see his response.

He understood with dawning gravity. "You mean, the young men lied?" he said, stopping on the sandy gravel.

"Yes. If what Alphonsine says is correct, and it was not Dai Tregarron who struck the young woman."

"It was not," he said, shooting a glance at Alphonsine then back again to Claudine. "I was witness also. I don't know who did strike her. I am not acquainted with the young men to know one from another. But Tregarron is older, and quite distinctive. He was standing apart from them, and it was not he."

Claudine drew in a deep breath. She did not dare to look at Alphonsine, whom she was about to embarrass profoundly, but there was no alternative to it.

"Mr. Barton, I wonder if you have

considered fully the consequences if you and Alphonsine were to tell the truth?"

"I know that they will fight against us, Mrs. Burroughs. In fact, they will do all they can to discredit us and prove that we are wrong. I don't know what motive they could ascribe to us. But Mr. Tregarron will lose his life if we say nothing, and that is not an acceptable bargain. No honest man would allow such a thing. I have only been quiet for this long because of Alphonsine." There was no pomposity in his voice. He was not proclaiming his virtue, simply stating what he believed to be a fact.

"Indeed. And *have* you considered what Miss Gifford may lose?"

Claudine said as softly as she could in the breeze and above the sound of their footsteps in the gravel and the gentle swishing of skirts.

John Barton was embarrassed and for the first time unable to find easy and passionate words.

Claudine said it for him. "Mr. Halversgate will not marry her."

"Well, it seems unavoidably true that either he knew who killed that poor woman — and he lied to protect his friend and thus blamed an innocent man — or else he killed her himself, possibly not intending to," Barton responded. "I hardly think her father would permit the marriage after that, whatever proves to be true."

Alphonsine turned away, hiding

her face from them both.

"You have not taken my point, Mr. Barton," Claudine said, hating doing it. "Mr. Halversgate will not marry her because she was keeping a tryst with another man, even if nobody believes you and he emerges with his reputation intact — and Mr. Tregarron hangs. Alphonsine's testimony will ruin her reputation, whatever happens."

Barton looked as if she had punched him in the stomach, knocking the breath out of his lungs. He stood still, not even fighting for words.

"It is likely no one else will marry her, after such a scandal," Claudine added. Would he accept this? Did he love her as much as apparently she loved him?

Barton looked ashen-faced, but there was no time for pity now. She stood her ground and waited.

"I would marry her the day she would have me, Mrs. Burroughs," John Barton said at last. "But her father would not permit it. He has already said so."

"If you testify against Cecil Crostwick, Creighton Foxley, and Ernest Halversgate, his opinion may change," Claudine replied. "He may no longer have a more acceptable choice." She drew in her breath to add that she hoped passionately that that had not been their intention from the beginning, then thought better of it. The thought was too ugly to bear. Instead, she added further weight to the other side. "And of course the families of the three young men, who have considerable power in both business and society, will not forgive you. You may pay a very heavy price for your honesty, Mr. Barton. I don't know what your ambitions are, but it might spell the end of them."

"Are you trying to dissuade me, Mrs. Burroughs?" he asked, his voice tight in his throat.

"No, Mr. Barton, I am trying to be fair."

"You have been fair, Mrs. Burroughs," he said gravely. "Now let us go and do what we have to. Whatever it proves, I believe the cost of silence would be greater, not only to Mr. Tregarron but to me."

Claudine hoped profoundly that he was right, but she did not say so. She simply nodded fractionally and smiled at him then looked at Alphonsine.

Alphonsine gulped. "I'm ready," she said huskily.

An hour later, damp and beginning to get a little chilled, the three of them sat in front of Oona Gifford. They were stiff with apprehension, struggling to keep their courage high.

"I think you had better explain to me," Oona said quietly after the maid brought in high tea and fresh toasted crumpets then departed. It was dark and late, far too late for such refreshments, but none of them had eaten since luncheon, and it was now past dinner.

Alphonsine looked at the man she loved, then at her mother, and finally at Claudine.

"One of you, please," Oona requested.

It seemed to fall naturally to Claudine to explain. She did so as briefly as was possible, detailing all the facts and what she believed was likely to happen as a result of both Alphonsine and John Barton going to the police and telling the truth, or their remaining silent and saying nothing. She left out none of the consequences, good or bad, certain or problematical. No one interrupted her.

"I see," Oona said at last.

Alphonsine stared at her. She looked lonely, frightened, and very young. It occurred to Claudine to wonder how long she had been without a mother since her own mother died, and then her father had met and married Oona. Perhaps too long for her to retain the power to believe that she would not be left inexplicably alone again.

Oona smiled. She reached out her hand and put it very gently over Alphonsine's where it lay on her skirt.

"You seem to have thought this over very carefully. Are you certain that it is what you want to do, even knowing the inevitable consequences? I think Claudine is right and they will be exactly as she says. Innocent or guilty, and whether he loves you or not, I don't think Ernest Halversgate will marry you when he knows this. Even if he wished to, I doubt his mother would permit it." A very slight smile touched the corner of her mouth then vanished again. In that instant Claudine knew that Oona was entirely on her stepdaughter's side, perhaps with more understanding than her own mother might have had. Maybe the fear for her was less. She had not loved her as a child and so did not in any sense still see her as one.

It was Barton who spoke. "I have already met Mr. Gifford, ma'am," he said gently. "He is aware of my feelings for Alphonsine, and he made it politely but very definitely clear to me that I am not suitable as a husband for her. I'm . . . sorry."

"That was then," Oona told him. "It looks as if circumstances are about to change rather dramatically. I shall speak to him. You will remain here in the withdrawing room. Finish the tea and the crumpets. Claudine and I shall go and discuss the issues and what may be done."

Claudine was startled. She was not a family friend and had no standing in the matter at all. Was Oona about to tell her so and dismiss her with all the outrage she had so carefully concealed until now?

As she followed Oona across the hall and along a wide passage to the door of Forbes Gifford's study, Claudine found her head spinning. She was afraid for a moment that the sheer tension of it would make her trip, even faint.

Oona knocked on the door. Without waiting for an answer, she turned the handle and went in.

Forbes Gifford was sitting by the fire with a book in his hands. The room was warm both in temperature and in the rich leather and velvet of its furnishings, the polished wood and the glowing carpet.

He looked up and saw his wife with pleasure. Then, the moment after, he realized she was not alone and rose to his feet, his face grave with concern. "Has something happened?" he asked.

As soon as Claudine was inside with her, Oona closed the door.

"Yes, my dear, I'm afraid it has. I could explain it to you, but I might do so a good deal less lucidly than Claudine will, if you will permit it? I'm afraid it cannot wait until a more convenient time."

"Very well, if this is necessary, then we had better proceed. May we offer you some refreshment, Mrs. Burroughs? You seem . . . a little damp. Are you chilled? Would you like the seat nearest the fire?"

Claudine accepted it. To tell the truth, she felt shivery. It was not the temperature in the house, it was her own nerves. At Forbes Gifford's insistence, she again told the story of the attack on Winnie Briggs and exactly what Alphonsine had told her. As she did so, Forbes's face darkened. Every so often he glanced at Oona, and she affirmed what Claudine said.

When she had finished, Claudine sat motionless, waiting for the storm to break.

"And do you believe him?" Forbes asked, looking at her through narrowed eyes.

She considered for a moment evading the answer but knew it would be futile. She knew exactly what he meant, and he would not appreciate prevarication.

"I do," she answered. "Of course, I wondered if it might be an elaborate piece of opportunism he had seized so that he could sabotage Alphonsine's chance to marry Ernest Halversgate, or anyone else of suitable expectations. But I believe that Alphonsine really did see the incident and that it was not Tregarron who instigated it or indeed struck the woman at all."

"And do you believe that my daughter was keeping an assignation with John Barton when the attack took place?" he pressed. "Have you any means at all of proving that she was there, and not somewhere else, where she should have been, entertaining our guests?"

"I have not tried to find proof," she admitted. "But I am sure you could question your own staff, if you wished to. What Alphonsine described to me was exactly what she would have seen from the neighbor's windows onto the terrace. I saw the same myself, from the other side, when I went out there a few moments after the attack. Mr. Tregarron had moved forward from the place Alphonsine saw him, in order to try to save the woman who was lying on the stones. Everyone else was exactly where she described them. Tell me, Mr. Forbes — you have known Alphonsine all her life — do you believe her to be capable of creating such a story in order to free a man she knows might be guilty of murder and condemn to scandal at least, the gallows at worst, three young men whose families are friends — all in order to ruin herself socially and marry a young man who has no money and few prospects that are of the order she is accustomed to?"

"I think she is young and in love and has no idea of the realities of life," he replied guardedly. "She has always been very comfortable, having all the clothes and parties she desires, all the friends, opportunities to do whatever she wishes. She can have no idea what it will be like to lose those."

Claudine drew in a deep breath and let it out softly. Now was the time to speak, however shaming, however difficult. She did it for Alphonsine as she might have done for a daughter of her own.

"Mr. Gifford, we all like certain luxuries. They are things we enjoy but could actually survive without. Most people do. One of the happiest women I know is married to a man who earned very little, in their earlier years together. She came from a good home where she could have married money, but she chose a man with a difficult past and a very doubtful future, because she loved him, and I think she was as certain as one ever can be that he loved her. They are now more than ten years after that decision, and I don't think she has regretted a day of it. She runs a clinic for street women, where I work quite often, and for which I am always seeking funding. That work brings me the greatest happiness I have."

Forbes Gifford stared at her, his attention total, although there were questions in his eyes that he was too sensitive to ask.

Claudine knew it was necessary she answer them anyway. It was difficult. She was ashamed to admit the truth, especially to people whose good opinion she would like to have had.

"I married a man who was suitable," she said quietly, "in my parents' view, after considerable thought. He appeared to be sober, honest, hardworking, talented, and likely to be faithful to me. He was all these things . . . I shouldn't speak in the past — he still is."

Forbes Gifford looked even more puzzled. She seemed to be making the exact point that he had, and the opposite of what she had implied.

She drew in her breath, let it out slowly, and tried to compose herself. Even so, when she began again, her voice was husky.

"He is also unkind," she told him. "He seldom criticized me openly to begin with, but it was always there in a remoteness, the praise of others in comparison with me, the condescending explanations of things I did not immediately grasp, and then afterward the reminder that he had taught me. I grew to despise myself and believe that I was displeasing to him, possibly to most people."

Forbes Gifford frowned but not at her. His eyes remained gentle and increasingly distressed by the story she was telling. She saw that there was no need to explain further.

"He did not love me," she said simply. "Nor did I love him. It is a long time since we shared anything with pleasure, or even with kindness. We do not laugh at the same things or admire the same moments of beauty. I wish him no harm, but I am happier when I do not have to see him or speak to him. I think it is possible he feels the same of me. Perhaps I am not even the quality of person I could have been, had I believed in myself and my own worth. Humility is a sweet virtue in anyone, but to be without faith or hope only destroys. It is much harder to find when you are unhappy."

She could see plainly in his face that she need say little more.

"Alphonsine is a lovely young woman, and I refer not to her face, which we can all see, but to her spirit. Please do not crowd her into doing something that she knows to be bitterly wrong in order to cement a marriage with a man who does not love her, nor does she love him. And if you are still intending to, believing it in her best interest for the future, consider that if he would lie and let an innocent man hang for a crime his friends committed, how well will he care for his wife, if it should in some way inconvenience him?"

"You have said enough," Forbes interrupted her. "It will be most unpleasant to do as you say, but there is no alternative that is acceptable. I thank you for your honesty. It cannot have been easy. Your own example makes the best argument you could for virtue over expediency." He glanced at Oona then back at Claudine. "Thank you. It shall be done as you suggest."

Claudine was too choked with relief, gratitude, a strange sense of freedom, to answer him.

"Well then, you'd better get on and deal with the rest of it, hadn't you!"

Squeaky said when she told him the next morning.

"The rest of it?" She was at a loss. "Alphonsine will tell the police — Sergeant Green, or whatever his name is — and they will withdraw the charges against Mr. Tregarron."

"If they believe her," he said dubiously, pulling his face into an expression of tortured doubt.

"We'll have to make it so that they do," she said, not quite sure what she meant. She could not bear to have come this far, and at such cost, and give up now. Was she absolutely sure it was the truth, sure enough to swear on oath? Sure beyond any doubt at all?

"Right!" Squeaky agreed. "Why should they?"

She lost her temper with him. She was tired and had been bitterly embarrassed telling Forbes Gifford so much that was painful in her own life. She had never put it into words before, and it had hurt more than she had expected. It was a story of absolute failure. Now Squeaky was doubting her, too, and in the place where she felt safer than anywhere else, even her own home.

"If you don't believe it, then I had better continue without you," she said angrily, starting to rise to her feet.

"Wait!" he said abruptly. "Don't go all soft on me now! I believe you, but you need the police to. I only want you to think about how

you're going to make that happen."
He looked at her with a slight
squint. "What's the matter with
you? You seem all . . . pushed out
of shape."

He was more perceptive than she
had foreseen, but she did not want
to tell him all she had revealed to
Forbes Gifford about her personal
circumstances. "I don't know how
to make the police believe me,
except that Alphonsine and Mr.
Barton say the same thing about
where people were, and it fits in
with what I saw."

"Then you'd better go and see if
Tregarron says the same," Squeaky
said flatly. "I'll arrange it."

She was incredulous. "How are
you going to do that? I'm hardly

family. They wouldn't admit me to his cell. And for goodness' sake be careful what you say. Don't you —"

He froze her with an indignant glare. Slowly he rose to his feet. "Where'll I find you when I've done it?" he inquired with raised eyebrows. "And don't ask any questions you don't want the answers to."

It was arranged the following day. Claudine was let into the prison and conducted to the cell where she would be allowed fifteen minutes with Dai Tregarron.

She had rehearsed in her mind several times what she would say to him. Each time it was different, and nothing was satisfactory, let alone good. She was so nervous her fingers were stiff. Her legs were a little wobbly, and she did not feel as if she could draw sufficient breath.

When Tregarron came in, he looked smaller than she remembered him, and somehow faded, as if dust and the harsh light had robbed him of luster. Above all, he looked appallingly tired, the lines in his face deep and the vitality drained away from him.

He stood in the doorway, unwilling to come in, and she knew he was embarrassed in front of her.

She hesitated for a moment then began. "I have very little time, Mr. Tregarron. Please come in and sit down so I may speak to you without having to raise my voice, and perhaps be overheard."

"If you are sorry for me, you don't need to be," he said, moving forward only a few steps. "And if you've come to save my soul —"

"I haven't," she said sharply. "If you want your soul saved, you will have to do it yourself. Of more immediate concern to me is saving your neck. That is, if you did not strike Winnie Briggs so hard that she died of the blow."

"I didn't," he said, taking another step toward her and putting his hands on the back of the wooden chair. "But nobody's going to believe that. It's either me or one of those fancy young gentlemen from well-bred and well-heeled families. Who do you think they're going to believe? For that matter, who do you think they can afford to disbelieve?" He pursed his lips. "Sorry, Olwen, you're off in some dream of your own."

"I haven't time to argue with you," she said impatiently. "Please sit down. You are making me stare up at you, and it is uncomfortable. I need to know exactly what happened. And, please, be precise."

"Why? It makes no difference now." He looked desperately tired, as if he had worn himself out thinking, struggling to untangle in his mind a knot that may only be pulled forever more tightly.

"There are two witnesses," she told him. "If what you say is the same as they do, then you will be believed. Now stop wasting what

little time we have, and tell me."
She did not add that neither Alphonsine nor John Barton had seen
who actually struck Winnie Briggs.

"Witnesses?" His eyes widened.
Hope was naked in his face, and
then the moment after, it turned to
disbelief. "No there aren't. There
was no one else on the terrace. If
there had been, they'd have said
something before now. There was
nowhere they could have been.
Someone's lying, for their own
reasons. It won't hold up in court."
His voice was edged with despair,
which was the sharper for the brief
flare of hope.

"They were behind a window, in
a room where they should not have
been. Now stop arguing and wast-

ing what few minutes there are. Do you want to hang for this?" She was being brutal, but she was afraid the warden would return for her any moment and it would be too late. "What happened?"

He swallowed as if there were something solid stuck in his throat. "I brought Winnie, because they wanted someone who'd be a bit fun," he began. "And honestly, I think they also wanted to shock a few people. They thought it would be amusing." He blushed very faintly; it was no more than a hint of color in his pallid cheeks. He caught her glance, both of disgust and of urgency. "We were laughing and generally behaving like fools. Winnie was good value. She had a sharp tongue, that one, and a ready wit. They liked her. Then Foxley wanted a bit more, wanted to kiss her, and she told him to wait. He thought she was putting him off, and he got more pushy. Crostwick stepped in, but he did it clumsily and it made things worse. Foxley was in a bad temper anyway, and then he thought Crostwick was above himself so he shoved him away, quite hard. That was when Halversgate got involved as well. And the wineglass broke. The shards like daggers."

His voice dropped.

"I told Winnie to get out of it, and she tried to, but Foxley caught hold of her. She pushed him away. I think she was scared by this time.

Foxley lost his temper and slashed out at her. He caught her hard with one of the shards, maybe harder than he meant to, and she went down. She hit her head, and she didn't move again. At first no one took any notice. They were busy getting angrier with each other. I tried to pull them off and get to her, but Crostwick hit me, pretty hard. Halversgate was terrified out of his wits and tried to do something, but Foxley hit him, too, and he staggered back."

He looked at Claudine with haunted eyes. "That gave me a chance to get to Winnie. I thought she'd just passed out, but when I tried to find a pulse, I couldn't. I think I was too scared to try properly. My hands were shaking like I had the ague myself. That was when you came out — so you know what happened after that."

"Thank you," she said with a warmth of relief surging through her. "That matches what the witnesses say they saw. You are perfectly certain that it was Creighton Foxley who hit her?"

"Yes."

"Have you already said so to Sergeant Green?"

"There didn't seem to be a point. They all said it was me."

"Well, I suppose they wouldn't admit it was them, would they?" She rose to her feet. "Thank you. I will find out exactly how we should proceed now. Keep hope, Mr. Tregarron."

"Flowers, white flowers," he said softly.

She turned at the door to stare at him. "What white flowers? What are you talking about?"

He smiled. "Where Olwen walks, white flowers spring up in the earth behind her."

Her eyes filled with sudden tears, and she banged on the door for the warden to let her out. She did not want Tregarron to meet her eyes again, in case he saw far too much in them. She was behaving like a fool.

Wallace was outraged. He stood in the middle of the rug in front of the fire and stared at Claudine as if

he could hardly believe what she
had said to him.

"It is absolutely out of the question! Have you taken leave of your
senses?" he demanded. "Have you
even the faintest idea what it will
do to our reputation if you launch
on such a preposterous course? I
don't know how you can be so
totally unreasonable. Who have you
spoken to about this? You make it
sound as if you have been telling
half of London."

"Forbes Gifford and Oona," she
replied lamely. She, too, was standing, and she would not sit down as
long as he was lecturing her as if
she were some obtuse schoolgirl. "I
had no choice in that, since Alphonsine is the witness who saw

335

what actually happened."

Wallace dismissed this with an abrupt jerk of his hand. "For heaven's sake, Claudine, she's a girl of — what is she, nineteen? She knows nothing. That's obvious by the fact she is prepared to throw away a perfectly good future with everything she could wish for, because she fancies she is in love with some young nobody who hasn't a penny to his name, but no doubt has a very ready eye on her fortune. Such a stupid girl is hardly worth listening to about anything."

"She is quite capable of recounting honestly and lucidly what she saw, as is Mr. Barton," Claudine said coldly. "As am I. What they describe is exactly what I found when I reached the scene. And it is, detail for detail, what Mr. Tregarron described."

"Indeed! And how do you know that?" he inquired, his eyes brilliant, challenging.

She had trapped herself. There was no escape, so she answered his question without excuse or evasion. "Because I asked him. There would be no point in speaking to the police if his account were different."

"You did what?" Wallace was aghast.

"I asked him," she repeated. "Is that not what you expected me to say?"

"I hoped I was wrong, that there was some other explanation." He shook his head as he spoke. "You seem to have lost whatever little sense you had. Do you even begin to grasp what you have done?"

It seemed to be a question to which he was expecting an answer, so she offered one, knowing it would be unsatisfactory. "I have given the police the evidence they need to clear an innocent man, and possibly charge those who are guilty."

"Don't be idiotic!" Wallace said furiously, his face purpling with anger. "You have meddled in matters that are none of your concern, and as a result you will ruin your own reputation and, more importantly, mine as well. And you will destroy young Foxley's life. He might have the friends and the influence to protect himself, but that remains to be seen."

He drew in his breath and continued. "You will, of course, also seriously damage Cecil Crostwick, and therefore his family, by implying that he lied in order either to cover his own part in the woman's death or to protect his friends. It will end Alphonsine Gifford's chance of a fortunate marriage. Halversgate can hardly offer for her now, when she has, by her own admission, had an indecent assignation with another man. In fact, no one of any standing will offer for her."

"It wasn't an indecent assignation," Claudine corrected him. "It was simply a meeting. The indecency is in your imagination. But I agree: Halversgate will not offer for her, because he now knows that he would not be accepted. He is both a liar and a coward, and Forbes Gifford would not have him for his daughter. Whether anyone else would offer remains to be seen; very probably not. But then, I think, she will be perfectly happy to accept Mr. Barton."

"Who has no means and no prospects," he said derisively.

"Perhaps it has slipped your mind that it is she who has the money, anyway," she said pointedly.

He sneered. "I am sure it has not slipped young Mr. Barton's mind!"

"He did not expect to marry her," she pointed out. "Or are you suggesting that this whole affair of inviting a street woman to the party and having Creighton Foxley lose his temper and beat her to death and Ernest Halversgate lie to protect him was entered into so Mr. Barton and Alphonsine could be conveniently placed to witness it? It was all a plot he invented for the purpose of creating a scandal from which they could benefit? Well, if Mr. Barton is clever enough to do that, then he should run for political office. He may well have ahead of him a bright future."

Wallace's face burned a deep plum red. "You have become absurd," he snarled. "I shall consult a doctor regarding the health of your mind. And I forbid you to attend

Mrs. Monk's clinic anymore. The place and its occupants have obviously affected your wits."

She had nothing left to lose. "Why? Is it really your judgment, Wallace, that if Tregarron drank too much and lost his temper with a street woman and hit her hard enough to kill her, then he should hang, but if, on the other hand, the exact same actions, in the same circumstances, were committed by Creighton Foxley, then that young man should be permitted to blame someone else? See another man hang in his place and walk away unscathed? That is your idea of what is just, and best for society? Would you also lie to ensure that this is what would happen? Or at the very best, turn a blind eye and pretend that you didn't know the truth? You sound like Ernest Halversgate: both a liar and a coward."

He swayed on his feet, his face mottled red.

"Please tell me that is not so," she continued. "I know we have little enough in common, less even than I used to believe, but still, I always knew you to have a sense of what was honorable. Am I wrong in that, too?"

He did not answer.

If she was going to add what was sharp in the forefront of her mind, then there would never be a better time than now. In fact, there might not be another time at all. So she burned the last of her bridges.

"You wanted a peaceful, comfortable Christmas, with all reminders of poverty, injustice, or other people's griefs well out of sight, so as not to disturb your pleasure. That isn't what Christmas is about, Wallace. Christmas is about offering hope to all people, not just those like ourselves. Christmas is about everyone: rich or poor, friend or stranger. The moment you exclude anyone, you exclude yourself." She was standing now. "I am going to visit Tolly Halversgate to see if she will help me persuade Ernest to face his responsibilities."

She walked out of the room, passing him without looking back. In the hall she told the footman to fetch her carriage and have it waiting for her in a quarter of an hour. She was quite aware of the lateness of the evening, and she did not care. Tomorrow morning would not be suitable to call upon anyone, and tomorrow afternoon would be too late. The family might be out now, but they would come home sometime. Claudine was prepared to wait.

She was fortunate, though. Tolly had decided to spend the evening at home, making her last-minute preparations for Christmas. She intended the dinner to be one the family would remember, including the various uncles, aunts, and cousins she had invited. She was startled and put to some discomfiture to see Claudine, but she could not think of any excuse not to receive her.

The dining room was already decked with garlands of holly and ivy and dark green pine. There were silver-tipped cones in a woven basket, dried flowers, and well-preserved shining autumn leaves in two huge vases. A pleasant perfume of cinnamon mixed with other spices hung in the air. The fire was burning, but low, because the weather was still absurdly clement.

Claudine was intruding almost unpardonably, but although it embarrassed her, it did not cause her to hesitate for a second, much less to change her mind.

"I am sorry," she said as soon as the door was closed and the footman's steps had retreated across the parquet floor of the hall.

Tolly forced a smile. "I'm sure you would not have come at such an hour without a good reason," she remarked.

"I'm afraid the reason is very good indeed, and urgent," Claudine responded, walking over to the other chair near the fire. She sat down without waiting to be invited.

Tolly followed because she had little choice. "What is it?" she said coolly, folding her hands in her lap.

"I will be brief. The very unfortunate quarrel on the terrace at the Giffords' party, in which the young woman, Winnie Briggs, was fatally struck, was witnessed from the window of another house. That has only just come to light, but now it is known exactly what happened."

Tolly's eyebrows rose in amazement. "My dear, Claudine, I really don't care! I cannot imagine why you should think I do, let alone at this time of the evening, three days before Christmas. If you think it is of concern to me, a letter would have been more than adequate." She gathered her skirts as if to rise.

"That would hardly be the act of a friend," Claudine said, remaining in her seat. "Or even of an honest person. You see, Ernest's account is quite seriously in error . . ."

Tolly froze, her body stiffening.

"I think it only fair to give him the opportunity to go to the police himself and correct it, rather than allow them to charge him with having given a false statement, which — as he has to be aware — will cause irreversible injustice."

This time Tolly did stand, her face white. "How dare you? What you are saying is preposterous! Who are these . . . witnesses? Why did they not come forward at the time? I don't believe you."

Claudine rose also. "Yes you do. Ernest was no doubt pressured into helping his friends, but he has been unhappy about it, because he is, for the most part, an honest man. If he goes on to lie under oath in court, he will have embarked on a path from which he cannot retreat. The guilt will be with him forever, corroding everything he touches from now on. He will have caused the appalling death of another man he knows is innocent. Will this not haunt him all the days of his life? If he marries and has children, what will he tell his family of this? Will he lie to them also? What will they think when they hear the truth?"

Tolly sidestepped the main issue. "Of course he will marry. He is shortly to become engaged to Alphonsine Gifford."

"She will not have him," Claudine replied. "Her father already knows that Ernest lied over who really struck the woman. And I doubt Ernest would want to have Alphonsine, when he hears that she is one of the witnesses."

Tolly stared at her, speechless.

"I'm sorry," Claudine said and was surprised by how seriously she meant it. She *was* sorry. Tolly had only the one son, and she loved him fiercely, if perhaps too protectively. Now just how vulnerable she was lay naked in her face.

"It is not too late to mend the situation," Claudine went on. "Ernest is at the point of a great decision in his life. Will he be the man he wishes to be, honorable and upright, even when being so costs a great deal of courage? It will not be easy, because I don't doubt the Foxleys will make this as difficult as possible."

"The Foxleys?" Tolly was not yet facing the inevitable.

"It was Creighton Foxley who

struck her, albeit not intending to cause her death. But he will still have to pay the price for it," Claudine explained.

"It can't be!" Tolly shook her head. "What about that Tregarron man? He's a drunkard and a womanizer!"

"So is Creighton Foxley," Claudine replied. "A little less far along the road, perhaps, but with a more violent temper. Ask Ernest if that is not true."

Tolly was still hovering on the edge of decision.

"Virtue is not always an easy or a comfortable thing," Claudine continued. "Sometimes it comes at a high cost. Perhaps that is one of the reasons we admire it. If Ernest

wishes to be what he seems on the
outside — I hesitate to use the
phrase 'pretends to be' — then he
must do more than speak well. He
must act well. Now, tonight, is the
moment for him to decide whether
he will speak the truth, even against
his peers, or whether he will lie to
cover their weaknesses. No — perhaps that is inaccurate. Alphonsine
has had the courage to speak out,
in spite of what it will cost her, as
has the young man she loves. And I
myself was there on the scene
within moments of the incident. We
will all speak as to what we saw.
Ernest's deceit will become public
knowledge. Knowing this, I'm sure
you will do all you can to see that
he does not make the choice to stay

silent."

Tolly blinked and shivered, staring at Claudine. "I realize that I do not know you at all, Mrs. Burroughs. You are frightening."

"Life is frightening," Claudine corrected her. "And beautiful and full of strange and unexpected opportunities. This is one of them."

"I will speak to Ernest," Tolly said in little more than a whisper. "I expect him home within half an hour."

"Good." Claudine smiled. "I will wait with you." She returned to the chair by the fire and sat down again.

Ernest did not struggle against the inevitable for more than a moment or two. The weight of the evidence against him was over-whelming, and the chance to play a hero too great to forfeit. He conceded, shamefacedly, that the truth was exactly as Alphonsine had said. If the fact that she was in love with another man distressed him, he hid it. Claudine believed that it was a greater wound to his pride than his heart, but he bore it with more dignity than she had expected.

It would also be a blow to his financial expectations, but he did not mention that at all.

She was not sure, but she had a strange feeling that some small part of him would be relieved to escape the imprisonment of his friendship with Creighton and Cecil. They would hate him for what they might well see as a betrayal, but there would be those who would respect him. At the very least, he would be free to be his own man: less daring, less outrageous, but a good deal truer to the best in himself.

The next day Forbes Gifford went with Alphonsine and John Barton to the station, and they offered their testimony as to exactly what they had seen on the night Winnie Briggs was struck. Claudine confirmed what she had found when she arrived on the terrace, which agreed with their account.

Then in embarrassment and some shame, Ernest Halversgate asked if he might amend his previous account of the incident and confess to what had really happened. Sergeant Green allowed him to do so and then to sign his statement.

When it was over, the charges against Dai Tregarron were withdrawn, and he was set free. As he walked out of the prison doors he met Claudine, who was not willing to accept anything as accomplished until she had seen it for herself.

He stopped in front of her, blinking as if he had only just seen the sunlight.

"Thank you," he said simply. "You believed in me more than I believed in you. It's a long time since anything like that happened."

It occurred to her to say something a little humbling, in case he imagined his charm had inspired her to do it. Then she saw the pain in his eyes, the self-criticism, and changed her mind. He did not need that kind of cautioning. He was already more than sufficiently aware of his own weaknesses.

"Don't do it again," she said gently. "I think we had a good deal of luck this time."

"I'll send you white flowers, Olwen," he said quietly. Then with a nod of his head, he turned and walked out into the street.

She would tell Wallace in time, but first she would go to the clinic in Portpool Lane and tell Squeaky Robinson. He deserved that, and quite apart from his deserving it, she simply wanted to share the moment with him.

She walked into his office and found him sitting at his desk, sheets of paper with figures spread in front of him, his fingers stained with ink.

"Well, what now?" he asked as she closed the door behind her.

"I just thought I'd let you know," she replied. "We did it. They withdrew the charges against Mr. Tregarron, and he is free."

Squeaky tried to keep a straight face, and failed. He could not keep the grin from spreading wide. He stood up and fetched a bottle of whiskey from the cupboard near the fireplace, and two mismatched glasses. He poured a good measure into each and passed one to her.

She did not even like whiskey, but

she took it anyway.

"Here's to you," he said with a deep sigh. "You got no sense at all, but all the courage in the world. Saved a man's life, you did, and gave him the chance to save his soul. Let's hope he takes it."

"Nonsense," she said briskly, but she knew her face was coloring with pleasure. "But I have learned something good about myself. I can stand up to people who have more power than I do, and fight for what I believe in." She took a large mouthful of whiskey and winced as the fire of it slid down her throat. The taste was indeed unpleasant. "Here's to Christmas," she said a little hoarsely. "And to the rebirth of dreams."

Squeaky shook his head in amazement. "Here's to you, Mrs. B." He emptied the glass in one gulp, and it slid down his throat like silk.

ABOUT THE AUTHOR

Anne Perry is the bestselling author of ten earlier holiday novels — *A Christmas Journey, A Christmas Visitor, A Christmas Guest, A Christmas Secret, A Christmas Beginning, A Christmas Grace, A Christmas Promise, A Christmas Odyssey, A Christmas Homecoming,* and *A Christmas Garland* — as well as the William Monk series and the Charlotte and Thomas Pitt series set in Victorian England and five World

War I novels. She lives in Scotland.

www.anneperry.co.uk